ALLE, ALLE, AUCH SIND FREI

Faith, friendship, family, football, freedom
Growing up in America in the 1960s

Paul Steichen

ONE

The Little Bird Fell Off Her Branch

This is my last year as a kid. Next year, I will be in high school. All signs pointed to a bright future and a good year for my class but when Sister Norbert fainted, the past stole our future, but then we stole it back.

Sister Norbert was teaching us Geography and suddenly started looking out the window. She stopped talking, kept looking, leaned back, and grabbed her throat with both hands.

She looked like she was having trouble breathing. I stood up at my desk and looked out the window too. I didn't see anything unusual. A big man was walking a big dog on a big leash. He must not have gotten the memo about dressing to fit the weather, which was ninety degrees and muggy. He had on boots, a long black leather jacket, and a thick belt on the outside of his jacket. He had an unusual way of walking. He held his left hand on his belt buckle and looked straight ahead. He looked like a robot. I don't think he had much fashion sense, but at least he should have dressed for the weather.

The last few days have been like living in a frying pan.

I guessed it must have been the heat that affected Sister Norbert.

When she fainted, she did not fall over as much as she just collapsed. All of a sudden, she was a heap on the floor. We all sat there hoping she would get up, but she didn't. I hopped up and went to get help. I went to Sister Mary Jude's classroom.

When I came into the room, she gave me the evil eye, so I blurted out, "Sister Norbert fainted."

She hesitated and then told her class, "No talking while I'm gone."

I followed her back to my classroom. When she saw Sister Norbert on the floor, she ordered me to go to the convent, get a pillow, and bring it to the office.

Away I went.

At the convent, Sister Damien answered the door. I told her Sister Norbert had fainted and I needed a pillow. Sister Damien was an elderly nun and didn't get the drift of what I said.

She asked me, "If Sister Norbert fainted, why do you need a pillow?"

"I don't need it; Sister Norbert needs it. Sister Mary Jude told me to get a pillow and bring it back to the office."

She went to get a pillow.

Sister Damien was famous for moving slowly. Once, Sister Norbert told me that whenever Sister Damien sees a fly, she likes to get her fly swatter and go after it, but her reflexes are too slow and the fly always gets away.

The other nuns get a chuckle over her lack of success.

They call her, "The Sister of Swat."

Maybe in her early days she was more successful when the dinosaur house flies were the size of pigeons and the stone fly swatters were deadly. By the time she got back with a pillow, I had cobwebs growing on me. I was thankful she didn't see any flies along the way.

I should have knocked when I got to the closed office door, but I didn't think of it. I opened the door and Sister Norbert was spread out on the floor without her habit on. I could see her arms, neck, head, and her bright-red hair. Sister Mary Jude had her sleeves rolled up and I could see her arms up to her elbows. I knew nuns had hands and faces, but anything beyond that was a mystery.

Somebody told me all nuns were bald.

Sister Mary Jude growled at me, "Give me the pillow and close the door quietly and go back to your classroom."

I gave her the pillow and saw that Sister Norbert's eyes were opening.

Sister Mary Jude was rubbing Sister Norbert's arm and saying, "Wake up, my little bird, wake up."

As I closed the door, I noticed that both of the nuns had numbers on their arms. They were on the inside of their left arm in a faded blue. Sister Norbert's looked like ZZ6135 but it was poorly written.

Nuns don't carry purses so maybe they write their phone numbers on their arms. If you found a nun walking around with amnesia, you could call the number on her arm. Sometimes people can be really clever.

I personally wouldn't have thought of it.

I never told anybody what I saw that day in the school office. If the Sisters of Providence at their home convent at St. Mary of the Woods College near Terra Haute find out I saw Sister Norbert's hair she might be in big trouble. She was by far the nicest of the nuns.

3

What I saw will remain a secret.

The number confused me until I remembered my first day at kindergarten. I don't remember this happening, but Dad teases me and says it happened. I went with Mom and Dad to meet the teacher the day before kindergarten started.

There was a woman sitting at a table in the gym and she asked me, "What's your name and where do you live?"

I answered, "Paul, and I live at Mom and Dad's house."

I guess I failed some kind of test because Mom laughed and told the woman my full name and our address. I knew our address but she asked me where I lived, not what is our address.

Dad kept laughing, "Doesn't even know his own address."

I told Dad I knew our address but he kept saying I didn't. The next day before I went to school, Mom wrote my phone number in ink on the inside of my arm. I didn't see any other kids with numbers on their arms, so I wasn't happy. It made me look like I didn't know my phone number and I was stupid. When I got home, I rubbed the number off and that was the first and only time I had a number on my arm.

TWO

Sister Skunk Fights Back

"Mr. Lyons, this is Sister Mary Jude. I hope I didn't wake you, but I think our prowler is back."

"Did anybody see him? I'll be right there so hold tight," he responded.

It was still dark. "Where's my holster?" he asked his wife.

"There's a prowler at the convent again."

She answered, "It's in the pantry where it always is unless it grew feet and walked away. This isn't World War II. The war is over and has been for years. We don't need the gun anymore. The police could be there in a few minutes. What if the prowler has a gun, too? I don't want you getting hurt for something that isn't your fight."

Mr. Lyons responded, "If a prowler is trying to jam the nuns, that's my fight."

He grabbed his .45 out of its holster and headed outside in his pajamas. Tony Lyons lived just two houses from the convent. A car ran the stop sign on Kenwood as Tony's dad skipped out of his house.

Sister Mary Jude watched from the upstairs and then called out when she saw Mr. Lyons, "Find anything?"

"Nobody's here—it looks like the front door got jimmied a bit, and by the way, what is that smell? I can hardly breathe," he cried.

Sister Mary Jude answered, "That's Sister Skunk. She's Sister Norbert's pet. The prowler must have attacked her."

"Smells to me like she attacked him! So, Sister Norbert has a pet skunk." Mr. Lyons was covering his nose and mouth with his hands.

"No, it's a wild skunk that comes at night and digs for food in the convent lawn. But Sister Norbert gave the skunk some grapes one night and now they're friends. Sister Norbert named her Sister Skunk because the skunk has a black and white 'habit.' Maybe there was a prowler and Sister Skunk didn't like what he was doing, so she sprayed him."

Mr. Lyon's eyes were burning as he replied, "I don't think skunks are that smart. I'll come back when the stink dies."

He was still barefoot and in his PJs as he ran back to the house and shrieked, "Good God, keep the windows closed! Sister Norbert has a pet skunk!"

Mrs. Lyons was standing by the door and suggested, "Maybe she should get a goldfish for a pet instead."

It was about 4:30 and still dark. I was just a block away on Capitol Street delivering Jamie Lanagan's Star newspaper route, when I heard someone running down Kenwood. Then a car door slammed and a car peeled out going toward 49th. I rode my bike over to see what happened. Other than the street lights, a few lights on upstairs in the convent, and Mrs. Lyons' kitchen light, the street was completely quiet and dark. A cloud of bugs flew around each street light and bats flew through, catching the bugs. It must be mating season for skunks, so I got back on my route quickly.

Tony later told me that his dad scared off a prowler at the convent. Tony's dad is still upset about what happened to the kids in Chicago at Our Lady of the Angels school. Ninety kids and three nuns were murdered by somebody who hates Catholics. The arsonist killer tampered with the fire alarm, so it wouldn't work and warn the kids. He started fires on both stairs so the kids upstairs couldn't get down. This was the worst mass murder in the history of Chicago. The killer got away.

Mr. Lyons told Tony, "It happened there, it can happen here."

I didn't think prowlers got up so early. I thought they came late at night when they are drunk. When you deliver in the dark, the money is great but in a way it's a real dangerous job by yourself. I am more the after-school delivery type.

The convent

THREE

The Ron-D-Vu Incident

I wasn't a good football player but I loved being on the St. Thomas team. Most of the guys in my class had started growing and some of them were almost the size of grown men. Tony was getting bigger and looked like Floyd Patterson, the colored boxing champion.

When Patterson held a workout before his title fight at the coliseum a few years ago, Tony and his dad went and ever since, Tony has loved anything and everything about Floyd. He even got a Floyd Patterson haircut and had pictures of him on his bedroom wall. If the light was just right, you could see a black mustache growing on Tony's lip. Wally was already as big as his dad. He could throw a left-handed curve ball and was known for his long-distance home runs.

I was still sporting an 80-pound weakling body on a massive 5´3″ frame. I also have a bad case of freckles which I need to get rid of before next year. I don't think freckles and high school go well together. Some people thought I was weak, but I wasn't. I just looked that way because I was too small for my age. I needed to grow.

This "stuck as a child" bit was getting old.

I played end on both offense and defense. On offense, we never did anything but run around end.

Tony, our quarterback, and Larry, our halfback, were very quick so we got big plays running around end. Mr. Lyons was Tony's dad and our coach. Tony was a good passer but he never threw a pass all year.

Nobody could stop our running game.

On defense, all I was supposed to do was keep the other team from getting around the corner and watch the back door for reverses. We didn't want done unto us what we were doing to others.

We practiced each day at Butler. Butler was a local university just a few blocks from St. Thomas. Having Butler was a fun part of the neighborhood. After practice, we would go across the street to the Ron-D-Vu. The "Vu" as we called it was a drive-in restaurant with car hops and a walk-up service window.

"Buzzing the Vu" was a popular teenage sport. A slow drive around to "see and be seen" was something I was really looking forward to when I got my driver's license, and also have a beautiful girlfriend by my side.

The popular drink for the bicycle set was a Suicide. It was a mix of all the sodas on tap. They put a plastic skull on the straw with a small rubber band for those with the courage to defy death by drinking a Suicide. Tony thought a Suicide was the way to go. Wally put his Suicide skulls on his bike handlebars.

I stuck with Coke.

Tony was in a laughing mood with his transistor radio in one hand and a Suicide in the other. The radio DJ introduced one of our favorite new songs, "The Monster Mash." Tony started to sing and dance along with the song. My favorite part of the song was near the end when Igor says, "Mash good." I loved that part. I was sitting on my bike eating French fries. Otherwise I would have been singing too.

I heard somebody yell, "Turn down that jungle music!"

I looked and saw a guy sitting in a Corvette and now he was yelling, "I said turn down that jungle music."

Tony heard him but ignored him. I walked my bike up to his car and said to him, "I don't think there are many jungles in Transylvania."

He looked at me and said, "What are you talking about?"

I told him, "That was an extremely intelligent statement on your part. I want to thank you for sharing it with me. Your mind is very impressive...for your species. You could be the next monkey in space for the Russians."

He came back by calling me "a little weasel."

I worked this guy pretty hard for two reasons.

First, I'm not fond of loudmouths insulting a friend, and besides I had my helmet and uniform on so I felt pretty tough.

And, second, I also had ten or fifteen teammates around the corner getting food. If this bigot would get out of his car thinking he could rough us up, he'd be making a big mistake. Wally and Tim and some other guys showed up.

Then I said loudly to him, "It's just great that you love jungle music."

Steam was coming out of his ears and I loved it.

"There's something wrong with you, kid," he shouted. Then he asked what school we were in and I told him St. Thomas Aquinas.

"So, St. Thomas A Candy Ass. Is that Catholic?" he said with a dentistless grin.

I came back with, "It's St. Thomas Aquinas, and don't put the name of my school in your dirty mouth."

He flicked a cigarette at me, but it missed and landed closer to Tony. Tony picked it up and pretended to smoke it.

Tony saw the cigarette was a Chesterfield and wanted to pounce and so he said to this dingleberry, "Forget Kools, I like to wrap my lips around a Chesterfield just like you do. It's been great sharing a cig with you."

Tony started to give the cigarette back.

The Chesterfield smoker motioned to Tony to stay back and sneered at Wally and me, "I would never go to school with spooks."

I answered back, "Let's be honest, you never went to school at all, did you?"

He was getting angrier and said, "You and your bugaloos sing real good. I'm going to remember you."

I returned the insult by saying to him, "We're going to try and forget you, so crawl back under your rock."

He started to back up and leave. I told him, "I know you from somewhere. Now I remember, you have that motel on the old highway. Wasn't it the Bates Motel? How has your mom been doing? I haven't seen her for a while."

He pulled onto 54th Street and gave us the finger. Somebody yelled at him, "Chuck you, Farley."

Wally added, "Cousins shouldn't marry." He kept giving us the finger.

I yelled, "Norman, come back." Then he laid some rubber and kept going.

Wally heard some engine misfiring and laughed, "What a doofus. Why have a nice car and not have it tuned properly? Mr. Chesterfield needs a tune-up."

Wally was a child expert on cars and dogs.

I felt I got one over on "Chester." He just got shown up by a kid in grade school. So I was happy. Tony was still upset and wanted to give Chester's face a tune-up.

The school

FOUR

Ottomatic Alarm

Sister Norbert was putting on her shawl to go to the rectory garage and feed the stray cat, Otto. Most people thought his name should be spelled "Auto" because he stayed in the garage. However, Sister Norbert told me she named him Otto because that was her father's name.

Suddenly, she heard a loud cat hiss. She looked out the window but in the darkness couldn't see much. The hiss turned into a shriek as she hurried up and left the convent. Was Otto in a cat fight? As she approached the garage, she saw a man leaving. In the darkness, she couldn't tell who it was.

"Hello!" she called to him, but he didn't stop.

So she turned her attention to Otto.

"Otto! Where's my boy? Where's my hungry boy?"

After a few more calls, Otto crawled out from under Father Munshower's car.

"Where's your bowl? Looks like somebody took your food dish."

Sister Norbert had been using a large glass ashtray from the Claypool Hotel as a food dish for Otto. There was cigarette smoke in the air.

She couldn't find Otto's dish so she looked around the dark garage for a spot to put the scraps she brought to feed him. The only place she could find that was clean was the shiny hood of Father Munshower's new car. So she put the food on the car hood and Otto jumped up and finally stopped meowing and started eating.

"This is our little secret, Otto. You need to be a member of the 'clean plate' club. But in this case it's the 'clean hood' club. Hopefully, Father Munshower won't ever know."

Otto is a particularly unattractive cat. His face is all scarred from his many fights. Both ears have chunks missing and his tail is broken. I wouldn't touch him but Sister Norbert pets him like he is beautiful.

He is a lucky cat.

Sister Norbert has a fear of dogs. As a girl she was bitten by one and now she freezes up when a dog gets near her.

Sister Norbert had barely returned to the convent when she saw Father Munshower leave the rectory with his car keys in his hand. He went through the open garage door, started his car, backed out of the garage, and moved under the spotlight outside the garage. At this point, he looked back and saw a strange hood ornament on his Dart. It was Otto eating. Father Munshower tooted his horn to scare Otto off his hood. Otto just kept eating. The nuns heard the horn and looked out upon this funny scene. Father Munshower turned on his windshield wipers to scare Otto off his hood. Otto just kept his head down and continued eating. After tapping the windshield and another horn toot, Father Munshower gave up and put his car into park and just sat there. The nuns burst out in laughter and enjoyed a good laugh at Father Munshower's expense.

FIVE

The Red Ball Express Rolls Again

Usually, I rode home from football practice with the colored guys since we all lived in the same direction. The only colored guy I would call a buddy is Tony. Earl, Larry, Buddy, and Raymond were cool and I liked them as classmates and teammates. The other colored guys are OK, or less. Tony and I were the top altar boys and we both liked to think and make plans.

Tony and I traveled between the white and colored neighborhoods. When we are in the white part of town, I have to protect him and when we are in the colored part of town, he has to protect me. I would help Tony on his paper route near his old house and every now and then some idiot would want to kick my ass for being white in a colored neighborhood. So Tony would step up and tell him to back off.

I step in when white people get stupid and lose their manners. If somebody insults Tony, I quickly insult them, even more so. Then they want to kick my ass, not Tony's. I then turn the bigot into a jerk and he looks stupid arguing with an eighth grader. Sometimes we just escape before things get ugly.

Tony has a fun family. His older brother Mike, plays halfback for Cathedral and is a gem. I hang a lot at Tony's. Tony's mom is a great

15

cook. When I eat dinner at Tony's if I don't like the food, I don't have to eat it like Dad makes me. If I don't understand or recognize the food, she cooks something special for me.

Dinner at my house is a torture chamber if Dad is home. Dad demands that you eat everything on your plate, no exceptions. If a dead bat fell on your plate, you would have to eat it. Dad eats everything—any part of any animal, anytime, anywhere. If you didn't finish everything on your plate, you had to sit at the table until 8:00, then go straight to bed. Sometimes, four or five of us wasted our evening getting punished for Dad's rules. Most of us were happy when we found out he wouldn't be there for dinner. When I had to do the dinner to bed treatment, I would wait until Dad was asleep, then sneak into the kitchen and eat.

Dad's eating rules turned all of us kids into magicians—we could make food disappear! If my sisters showed up for dinner wearing sweaters with pockets on a hot summer day, I knew a bad, bad meal was heading our way. When Dad was not looking, we would stuff the bad food into our pants pocket or into a sweater pocket, into a sock, spit it into our napkin, or the oldest Steichen Family Dinner survival trick, throw the food onto the floor under the table.

We did this for years until one of my sisters messed up. One day during a really bad meal, she threw a big piece of fat under the table and hit Dad's foot. The floor was loaded with food. Usually, we would come back later and clean up under the table to maintain our secret.

Dad blew his top.

We all had to sit there and then straight to bed. Later, when Dad started snoring, it was like the lunch whistle just blew at the Ford plant. The kitchen was full of silent, hungry kids lined up at the toaster or making a bowl of cereal or a peanut butter and jelly sandwich.

In a way Dad and I get along, but in another way we don't. When Dad is in town I spend more time with him than any of the other kids. Every Saturday I have to work at his warehouse cleaning vending machines until about noon, then I was his caddy for the rest of the day. Dad likes to see me working and normally I don't mind work if I get paid. Usually during golf weather I would caddy again on Sunday.

In a way, I'm more Dad's employee than a son.

I look at Wally's dad and Tony's dad and both of them are interested in what their sons are doing and thinking. I doubt if Dad remembers what grade I am in.

Wally's dad and Tony's dad are proud of their sons and say nice things to them about them. My dad likes to compare me to one of his friend's sons who Dad thinks is sharper than me.

Dad would say things like, "Mike Meany had a real cute girlfriend," then point out that I don't have one.

Dad acted like Mike was somebody special and I came up short by comparison. I know Mike and it boggles the mind that Dad thinks he is better than me. Mike Meany is a perfectly average guy. I have a lot more to offer, but Dad doesn't see it that way. I'll admit I'm not as average as he is. One thing about Dad is he will never change, so you might as well just accept how it is. He isn't a bad father, but honestly he doesn't care much for his kids.

As the fall kept falling, it got that we were riding home in the dark if we went to the Vu after practice. Some guys went straight home after practice and skipped the Vu to avoid riding in the dark. At one point, only Earl and I went to the Vu. Earl was always hungry because his mom was sick and couldn't cook any more. I had to eat in case dinner was bad and Dad was home. My next chance to eat might be 10 or 11. Earl and I had a lot of the same problems but for different reasons.

He's too big and I'm too small.

Two years ago, Earl and I were the top runners for our 100-pound football team. Last year, Larry replaced me because he had gotten bigger and better than me. This year Earl missed the weigh-in weight by two pounds and couldn't be a runner. In his mind, Earl is a runner like Wally is a pitcher. Due to my lack of size, I have to be happy that I am still starting. I'm already a has-been at thirteen.

I feel sorry for Earl that his mother is in the hospital. I told him that they don't let children visit their mother. But for some reason they let him visit his mom. I asked Meem, my grandmother, how come he can visit his mom in the hospital when she is there, but when Mom is in, we can't. Meem says my Mom goes to a different part of the hospital.

When Mom gets feeling bad, she locks herself in her bedroom and the kids are told to leave her alone. Meem shows up and is in charge until Mom feels better. Dad is gone most of the time making money as a traveling salesman selling Stoner vending machines. Meem told me that during World War II the pressure of having Dad bombing Germany and possibly not coming back, stressed out Mom. Her high school boyfriend from Dubuque was already killed in action.

She worried that Dad was next.

Even now, Mom gets confused when Dad is gone. She thinks he is back bombing the Nazis. After a couple of months, Mom comes out of her room and we can see and talk to her again. We haven't seen her since school started. I can't remember Mom not being around for Christmas.

Earl can't understand how Mom wants to avoid her kids. His mom is the opposite. She acts like her kids are her world.

When my Mom feels good, she is very funny and a good mother.

Last week in the middle of the night, I went down the back stairs to get something to eat and I saw Mom standing in the kitchen eating something. I was looking through the cracked door. It had been months since I had seen her. I knew I should have left her alone but I couldn't help myself.

I said, "Hi, Mom."

She looked at me with just one eye then turned away from me. She showed me her back and didn't want to look at me or talk to me. I hoped she would be happy to see me, but I was wrong. I backed up and left. At least I knew she was alive. Earl's mom could die if she doesn't get better. Earl thinks I got it bad and I think he's got it bad. After a few more weeks it was dark when practice ended, so we all went to the Vu before heading home. Our season was going great guns and practice was a lot of fun.

Everybody has had idiots yell something at them as they drive by. But I never had things thrown at me or have cars act like they are going to run me over and turn away at the last minute. I never thought there were so many active bigots in town. I thought these attacks were aimed at the colored guys only and I felt they were getting screwed by these jerks. A car pulled up to us and threw a Coke bottle at me. I could see in his eyes, he was aiming at me.

For a while, I felt some fear over being a target, but I talked to myself and now I don't mind. Next time, I'll get the bottle and throw it back. We started to ride our bicycles on the sidewalk, not the street. We rode in a line front to back. Tony called us the Red Ball Express because we were like a line of trucks. Mr. Lyons drove for the Red Ball Express in World War II. The Red Ball Express was the name given to the colored truck drivers who delivered battlefield supplies to the fighting troops. Tony told me his dad doesn't talk much about World War II.

He once told Tony, "I didn't join up to drive a truck."

Tony found out that Mr. Lyons got in trouble for leading an unauthorized raid that freed some people the Nazis were going to kill. Some of Mr. Lyons' colored buddies were killed in the raid and Mr. Lyons felt bad about it.

When we left the Vu, we pretended that we had to get through a

Nazi-held area to get home. We rode hard and fast and it was fun and much better than riding on the street and waiting for someone to do something strange. I think some people get courage and bad ideas at the same time.

My friend, who met Tennessee Ernie Ford at the State Fair, lived here.

SIX

Mr. Sauerkraut

Wally talked a lot about a new dog on his paper route. It was his favorite breed, a German Shepherd. Wally already had Sammy, a Border Collie, who is a great dog. I think Wally wants a tougher looking dog for protection. I couldn't have a dog so sometimes I wished I had an older brother to give me some protection in the neighborhood. Guys might not screw with me if they were worried about having to deal with a big, bad, older brother. My friends with older brothers told me it doesn't work that way. An older brother is a real nuisance and you still have to deal with the thugs on the street. Wally loves dogs. When he went with me to visit my grandma in Dwight, he always wanted to see my uncle's three Boxers. The smart one, Scrapper, used to follow the milkman, open the milk box, grab a bottle of milk with his mouth, and take it home to drink. You couldn't let him out in the morning or he went on his milk run.

The first time Wally saw the new Shepherd, the dog was chained to a tree inside a fenced yard. The Shepherd was caught up in the chain, choking. Wally, without thinking, jumped over the fence and unhooked him and the dog licked him in gratitude. Then, he even gave him his burger, fries, and Suicide. Wally put him back on the chain after he straightened it out.

After he was done with his route, Wally came back to check on the dog and saw somebody in the house. When he walked onto the porch, he was sure the owner would thank him for rescuing his dog and maybe even subscribe to the paper. Wrong, wrong, and more wrong.

A man answered the door and Wally introduced himself. He started telling the guy about rescuing his choking dog.

"I was riding my bike and I saw your dog caught up in his chain. I thought he might need help, so—"

The guy cut Wally off.

"If my dog isn't smart enough to keep out of the chain, let him hang. If he ever got off his chain, the only one needing help would be you. He is trained to go for the face in a fight. If he ever gets soft like your 'purse' dog, I'd shoot him in the head and throw him in a trash can where he belongs."

Wally went into kind of a shock and shot back, "What do you mean, 'purse' dog? Sammy will kick your fat ass, and besides, who gives you the right to shoot any dog?"

The fat ass demanded, "Get off my porch or I'll have you arrested for trespassing. I'm a good friend of Officer Tode. I don't need your lip, Junior."

The locked screen door gave this punk a drunken courage.

"You're right there," Wally sneered. "A chicken like you don't need any lip because you have a beak and feathers."

There wasn't a peep out of Wally's "fowl" as he slammed the wooden door.

Wally yelled one more insult through the door, "You're just a two-legged fart who smells like stale sauerkraut."

Wally left the porch and from then on called this walking fart, Mr. Sauerkraut.

After he left the porch, Wally secretly went around where the dog was chained. He and Sammy jumped the fence and greeted the German Shepherd. The dog begged Wally to pet him. The Collie and the Shepherd touched noses. Wally vowed to get this dog away from Mr. Sauerkraut. Wally left with his face intact and a new friend.

SEVEN
Things Change Quickly

Things can change quickly. Usually, I think it is smart to avoid fights but if I get mad enough I quit thinking and don't mind fighting. If I feel my head and neck getting hot I know my brain is about to go into neutral and my mouth goes into overdrive. I never start a fight but always fight back.

Or at least my mouth does.

I was playing with friends during recess when for no reason Bubbles tripped me. Bubbles was a tough kid who was bigger, stronger, and meaner than me. I had never had a beef with him, so I was shocked when he attacked me like that. Both of my hands were hurt when I hit the ground and one of my knees had a lot of skin torn off. I looked up and saw Bubbles laughing at me and muggin' for his friends. I went from shock and feeling pain to anger in about a second! Before I knew what happened, I jumped up, tackled him, got him on the dirt and had him in a headlock. All that time he spent laughing gave me an opening. I now had him in a headlock that can really hurt your head.

Once I had Wally in this hold, and by mistake I knocked him out! I thought I might have killed him, and so I threw three glasses of water on his head to revive him. I was so happy when he came around. When Wally's mom asked me how the living room rug got wet, I made up some story. I didn't want to tell her I almost killed her son.

I had to put a lot of pressure on Bubble's eye socket to keep him from getting loose. If he got away, he could drop kick me most of the way downtown and my face would end up like a Pasquale pizza.

He yelled at me, "When I get loose, you are a dead man!"

I was really mad and yelled back, "Well, then you won't get loose."

I threatened Bubbles by saying, "This is how Popeye got started," as I tightened my bony little arm into his eye socket.

I was still red hot.

I knew that I was hurting him as he was screaming from pain and frustration.

I could feel he was losing his strength. "You give?"

He grunted something that didn't sound like "I give," so I put more pressure on with my "arm" vice.

I could hear people yelling, "Bubbles and Steichen are fighting!"

He started to panic and I expected him to pass out any moment. Then the recess bell rang and I had to let him go. His head was red, his nose was running, and he had been crying from the pain. He had a hard time talking, but told me he'd see me after school.

I was still hot and told him, "Sounds great, we'll pick up where we left off, with me kicking your ass."

Later, Sister Mary Jude came up to me and asked what happened. I told her we ran into each other by mistake and it was no big deal.

As I sat in class that afternoon, I started to calm down. It's then that I realized after school I would have to refight Bubbles. It didn't look like a good setup for me. When I was completely calmed down, I knew I was in big trouble. By the "law of the playground," Bubbles wanted revenge for the pain and insult I put him through. He was a tough guy who couldn't have his badass reputation tarnished by a shrimp like me. I was hoping he was done with fighting, but he wasn't. When the fight resumed, I lost the "after school" part. Some said our fight was racial, but it wasn't.

To me, it was more a matter of what makes you laugh. Bubbles thought seeing me in pain was funny. I didn't share his sense of humor.

The next day in class, we both had only one good working eye.

EIGHT

The Revengeful Nun

Sister Norbert had always been nice to me and Sister Mary Jude had never liked me. I can't tell you why for either of them. Sister Norbert was like a fun older sister and Sister Mary Jude was an unhappy aunt. Sister Mary Jude is still mad at me for what happened during the Stations of the Cross when the archbishop was here last Lent. Some people laughed out loud when I fell and slammed into the archbishop before I hit the floor, so she thinks I showed up the archbishop—and that it was bad manners to touch the archbishop.

Last Lent, Tony, Wally, and I were altar boys for the Station of the Cross. It was a special visit by Archbishop Schulte to say the Stations. The service began at 11:30 a.m. and I was already very hungry.

When I was kneeling at the altar, I felt the first wave of bad feelings. I loosened my collar and tried to breathe better. I was OK for a while but then another wave came over me and everything turned grey and I almost fell over. I kept trying to get my bearings. I was able to stand up and walk as we left the altar and started the Stations. I got through the first two stations but I was having trouble seeing and breathing. I was leading with the big gold cross. Tony and Wally had candles and then came the archbishop. We stopped at the station and the archbishop moved in front of us and was about to announce the third Station when I got another rush that made me feel like I was being electrocuted.

I started to blank out.

I gave the cross to Tony and that is the last thing I remember. Tony said I just stood there glassy-eyed.

The archbishop in a loud voice announced, "The Third Station—Jesus falls the first time."

And that is when I fell; I fell forward and bounced off the back of the archbishop on the way down. Some of the people and a lot of the kids started laughing out loud. I was grabbed by the wrist and dragged out of the church by Wally's mom and another woman. Father Munshower thought it was a funny story and didn't blame me. Sister Mary Jude thought it was another example of me being a smartass, and because of my bad health arrival, most likely I had put the survival of the Catholic Church in jeopardy.

The strangest time I ever had with Sister Mary Jude was one day on the playground when I was playing with Tony.

We were making up jokes in pig Latin and Sister Mary Jude came over to us and said to me, "Mauchen, I told you to be quiet and if you had to talk, speak only French. If you can't stop coughing and talking in Yiddish or German, the nuns are going to make me leave you behind."

She started tearing up and left. I think I just ended up in her nervous breakdown. Tony was there, too, but she didn't even look at him.

Sometimes Tony, Wally, and I pretend like we can speak German for fun but I can't actually speak German more than a sentence or two at a time. I do know a lot of German words and Sister Mary "Rude" just called me a mouse. She has no manners. The only thing I know about Yiddish is you write it backwards. I do have a bad cough but why is that any sweat off her back. It's getting to be straight jacket time. Sister Mary Jude and Sister Norbert came to St. Thomas last year.

On the first day of school, Wally told me, "Sister Mary Jude was watching you like a hawk."

She told Sister Norbert that you are a "double ganger".

I asked Wally if that's better than a "single ganger". As always, I did not have a clue about what Sr. Mary Jude was saying. He told me she couldn't take her eyes off me. I was happy seeing my classmates again and didn't notice her noticing.

Last week, I was walking with Sister Norbert, and Sister Mary Jude came up behind us.

She pushed me aside and asked Sister Norbert, "Is this little 'wisenheimer' bothering you?"

For a nun, Sister Mary Jude had pretty poor manners.

I answered, "I would never bother Sister Norbert and you know that."

I guess I wasn't supposed to say anything so now she blew her top.

"Don't tell me what I know. You've mouthed off for the last time."

She grabbed Sister Norbert and went to the convent. I knew I was screwed, blued, and tattooed.

I tried to beat the phone call home. I hoped when I got home my Mom would be in a good mood listening to her Gilbert Bécaud French records. If I could tell my side of the story before Sister Mary Jude "poisoned" the well against me, I stood a chance. When I came around the garage, I saw Mom standing at the back door, waiting for me. She didn't look like she was going to be giving me the "Eighth Grader of the Year Award." Mom yelled at me to go back and apologize to Sister Mary Jude, or I was going to be kicked out of St. Thomas.

"For what," I asked.

"For bothering Sister Norbert."

"What!" I was speechless.

Mom barked, "If you don't go back right now and apologize to Sister Mary Jude for sassing her and promise to leave Sister Norbert alone, you're out of St. Thomas. There's nothing I can do."

I couldn't believe what I was hearing, so I told her, "There is something you can do. You can stand up for me! I didn't do anything wrong. She's a jerk, jerk, and more jerk."

Mom informed me, "I'm not going to argue with you. If you want to stay at St. Thomas, then go beg to stay. Otherwise, you're on your own."

I couldn't really figure out how things got so bad so quick. Mom probably is wrong and I have already been kicked out, so this is more a matter of rubbing it in for Sister Mary Jude's pleasure. I headed back to the convent to pretend I was sorry. I decided to bite my lip and admit everything was my fault because I was such a pathetic person. Of course, Sister Mary Jude delighted in talking about my extensive shortcomings. What a rich topic for her! I was told I was a pathetic loser and halfwit. I tried to not let any of this get me down.

I was just a dead bird being played with by a cat. Throw me up in the air and see if my wings flutter on the way down. There might be some life that needs to be crushed in me still. I came within a whisker of telling Sister Mary Jude my apology was just Hollywood acting.

In a way I thought, "Go ahead and kick me out, I'm tired of you, too." She acts like Smeiser, a neighborhood bully.

Sister Mary Jude tried to prolong my time on the rack, so I was sent home without knowing my fate.

She told me, "I'll call your mother when I decide."

On the way home, I got madder and madder. Mom was in the kitchen when I got home and she asked me what happened.

I answered, "I don't know. She will call you later. When she calls, tell her I am strapped into the electric chair and I want her to turn the juice on full blast and keep it on until my eyes pop out and my hair catches fire."

Mom scolded me by saying, "That attitude won't get you anywhere." I answered her, "I am already nowhere, I'll just stay here." I went upstairs and laid on my bed. I fell asleep with my boots and jacket on.

Later, Mom woke me up and told me I was still in St. Thomas.

The DAR

NINE

The Fighting Acorns

Most of the guys who got into a lot of fights, and all the neighborhood bullies, had bad fathers. Some of those fathers were mad all the time and some could explode like a volcano. Thank God, my father isn't that way. He only knocked me out once and I probably deserved it. Mom says Dad came home from the war and did a lot of drinking. On hot summer nights he likes to sit outside on the front porch, shirt off, beer in hand, working on his moon tan, lost in his own thoughts. You could tell he was back in World War II bombing the Nazis. Tony and Wally have nice dads. Most of my friend's fathers fought in World War II and many of them were tough guys and were scary to be around, especially if they were drunk. Some of them punched my friends, hit their sisters with wire clothes hangers, and slammed their wives up against the refrigerator. The kids who got beat up at home took their unhappiness to the neighborhood and shared it.

All of the playground fights at St. Thomas were the same. If it was two white guys, the fight was a wrestling match. Most likely one of the fighters would be a lunatic whose goal was to inflict as much pain as possible on the other guy. Usually this was a bully who didn't care if he won. All he wanted to do is hurt the other guy. Hurting people gives a bully a strange happiness. These bullies fight like animals. Most colored guys fought with some honor like men. If a colored guy felt the need to fight, the fight started quick. White guys, on the other hand, liked to announce their intentions. Colored guys just got to it. If you fight a colored guy, be ready quick.

If it was two colored guys fighting, it was a boxing match, and the goal of the fight was to outclass the boxing skills of the other—basically to beat the hell out of the other guy, while showing a cool profile. Two colored guys would fight to prove a point, then the fight stopped.

Most colored/white fights never got going. The colored guy would stand upright punching. The white guy was crouching down low trying to avoid getting punched and trying to tackle his adversary. The colored guy would step in and throw a few punches, then back up quickly to avoid being grounded.

Winning a fight is no big deal but losing one can be. In a fight you need all your strength at once and it can drain quickly. When you get in a fight, you get a lot of tension in your body which makes you tire quickly. After 10 to 15 hard thrown punches, a St. Thomas neighborhood boxer was sweating and breathing hard. His punches didn't have much sting once his arms got heavy.

About the same time, fatigue is setting in on the white fighter, who has spent the first part of the fight hunched over trying to avoid getting punched and trying to get a tackle to start the wrestling match. So far, all he's done is chase the boxer's feet and get socked in the head a few times.

The boxer isn't boxing and the wrestler isn't wrestling.

Often, interracial fights get off to such poor starts, they never get going. They end up with a lot of huffing and puffing and name calling and an unhappy mob cheering for a better fight.

My strangest fight was a two-slap thing with a girl when I was in sixth grade. I was having a minor disagreement with a girl named Hortense on the playground over something, when she slapped me on the face.

Without thinking, I slapped her back on her face. If she was one of my sisters, I could expect a harder return slap, an attempt to scratch out my eyes, and a few kicks. Unfortunately, she wasn't one of my sisters.

Hortense fell to the ground and started bawling and wailing, "Steichen hit me."

Either she's never been slapped before or she's trying to win an Oscar. She kept up her victim act until Sister Mary Jude took both of us to the office. When Sister Mary Jude found out she slapped me first, I got to leave. As far as the nuns go, I didn't have a problem but I still had a big problem—her older brother, Bobby, who was in eighth grade.

I was afraid he would want some family revenge on me. A few days later I saw Bobby and decided to get it over with, so I went up to him to see if an apology can stop a fight.

I started, "I'm sorry for what happened with Hortense."

"I'm not," he answered.

"I wish you would have knocked a few teeth out of her smartass mouth. I wish I could slap her myself but she's 'daddy's little princess' and she gets away with murder at my house. Steichen, you made me so happy when I saw her crying. Let me thank you." And we shook hands.

It wasn't the ending I expected. You never know what's coming down the pike.

TEN

Gridiron Glory

On the bus ride to our championship game, we started to guess who was the toughest man who ever lived.

We came up with eight choices:

Davy Crockett
Dick the Bruiser
Floyd Patterson
Al Capone
Moses
Steve McQueen
Blackbeard the Pirate
The David who killed Goliath (nobody knew his last name, possibly, David House)

We started to vote and it looked like Blackbeard the Pirate was going to be our choice. Blackbeard lit his beard on fire when he was fighting and after they chopped his head off, they threw his headless body overboard and it swam around the ship twice before disappearing.

Blackbeard didn't let the fact that he didn't have a head slow him down.

But right at the end, Tony spoke up for Moses. He pointed out all the different things Moses could do.

Tony said, "Moses could outthink anybody. He played the Pharaoh for a fool, threw poisonous snakes at him, and told the Pharaoh, "If you screw with my family, I'll screw with yours."

And you don't want to get on the bad side of Moses as that Egyptian found out. The big rule when dealing with Moses is you might be in the middle of a desert now, but don't chase him and his people if you can't swim. We wondered what Moses was like as an eighth grader. Then, we pulled into the parking lot and went all the way to the gate.

The St. Thomas Tigers have arrived.

The St. Thomas Tigers were one of the four teams in the Catholic Youth Organization or CYO football championship. If we were to win our first game against Holy Angels, we needed to play well. Coach Lyons told us they were tough and super-fast. Their star runner was a speed burner named Mike Blinkeye. Coach Lyons said Blinkeye is as fast as "greased lightning." Holy Angels is an all colored school that plays a lot like us. Their main play was a sweep around end with the occasional flanker reverse. Their quarterback, named Harold Dana, was fast but Blinkeye was faster. Like us, Tony was fast but Larry was faster.

My assignment was to keep them from getting around the corner on my side and to stay put in case of a reverse. Tackling Blinkeye was like shooting at a flying bird. If you shot where the bird is, it's already gone and you missed it. You had to guess where he would be and get there before he ran past. I had some success on Blinkeye, forcing him wide. One time he had me beat, and, luckily, I swiped at his foot and tripped him. Otherwise, long gone. I always got a tingly feeling when I saw the Holy Angels' backfield turn toward me and pick up speed with a road runner like Blinkeye bringing up the rear. He's a sharp number that can only be bottled up for so long.

We played well but near the end of the game we trailed by two points after Blinkeye blocked a punt and we recovered in the end zone for a safety for them. With just a couple of minutes to go we recovered a fumble on our 25-yard line. Our first play sent Larry to the right. No gain. Then, Larry to the left. No gain. Tony called our last time out and went to talk to his dad.

Basically, we needed something special or we would lose. We huddled and were waiting for Tony's return. I looked over at Larry and saw he had blood all over his chin and his jersey. He wiped his nose with the back of his hand and smeared bright-red blood all over his hand.

He was trying hard to catch his breath and didn't notice the blood.

I told him, "Larry, you've got a nose bleed."

He felt his nose with his hand and got blood dripping into his palm.

He looked a little scared and asked, "What should I do?"

Somebody told him, "Ball up some grass and jam it up your nose until the bleeding stops."

A couple of guys helped Larry get some grass balled up and stuffed up his nose. Some blood leaked through his grass plug but Larry was ready to go.

Tony came back to the huddle and said, "Dad says halfback sweep to the right."

My jaw just dropped as I looked at Larry. He still had blood coming out of his mouth and nose.

He heard the call, nodded his head and mouthed the word, "OK."

Larry had a lot of courage. I couldn't hold back.

"Tony, we need something better than that. They are expecting it. We need a trick play or we've lost."

Tony went into deep thought for a second and announced, "I have a play that will win us the game."

To my shock, he called a pass play to me. This was our first pass of the year. I ran my route and was wide open. Tony threw me a perfect pass—if I was 10-feet tall. I touched the ball but had no chance of actually catching it. Tony must have been under pressure, to make such a bad pass. I bet he felt terrible.

We got back to the huddle and Tony said, "Now for our game winning play."

Actually, I thought we had just tried that. "Punt position, Earl. You want to be a hero. Run left with the ball instead of punting it. Let them think we don't know what to do."

If Earl can win the game for us, it will make up for a lot of bad news he's gotten into since school started.

At the beginning of the season, Earl's mom was our best fan and she was a great mom and a lot of fun. She cheered for all the guys, not just for Earl. She was a dietician at an old folk's home and she was always talking about food. Even her homemade cheers were about food.

She would make up cheers like these: "Come on St. Thomas, it's time to put the pot roast on the table ... Time to crumble their cookie ... Put some relish on that hotdog and leave it in the end zone ... Bless us, O Lord, with a touchdown," and my favorite, "You got 'em now, St. Thomas, their potatoes are getting cold. Don't let them pass the gravy." At the end of the game, everybody was hungry.

Earl had quit the team when he missed the weigh-in weight to be a halfback. He was our best runner last year but missed by two pounds this year. His mom talked him back on the team. Earl was basically a calm guy but with the weigh-in failure and now his mom is in the hospital, he's wound tight and really not happy.

Tony continued, "Tommy, give Blinkeye a direct shot at Earl and at the last minute, close the door. Everybody listen! Get set on 'one,' but I'm going to talk before calling 'two.' Be prepared and hold your stance. "Earl, once you score, keep the ball. We're going to give it to your mom. We don't have flowers so maybe our victory football will cheer her up."

After hearing this, Earl was uncatchable. Blinkeye and Dana can be the best runners in the state of Indiana but they won't catch Earl with his Mom's "Victory, Get Well, Football."

We got set to punt. Mr. Lyons was jumping up and down yelling, "Don't punt, don't punt."

Tony called "one," we got in our stances, and then he said to me, "We need a fumble, so hit the returner hard, and we can still win."

One of Holy Angels players yelled back at Dana, their return man, "They want a fumble!"

Other than me, Tony is the best thinker I know. Now, he proved it. Right before starting the play, Tony announced in "pig" Latin, "No block this time."

Before Holy Angels could translate, he called "two."

The ball was hiked to Earl and Tony started to yell, "Fumble, on the ground, fumble, on the ground, fumble, fumble!"

Earl did some nice acting by bobbling the ball and then he flew past me. When the Holy Angels receiver, Dana, didn't see a punt coming, he bit into Tony's fumble talk and moved up to get into the action. It was too late to catch Earl now. Tommy closed the door on Blinkeye and tipped him over. In the confusion, with all the talk about a fumble, Earl was beyond reach when they started chasing him.

I just kept yelling, "Forget it, he's gone!"

I was more right than I knew.

Earl ran into the end zone, cleats a blazin'. Then he kept running out of CYO Field and down 16th Street toward St. Vincent Hospital. He wanted to deliver our victory football to his mom while it was still hot. One thing about Earl, he lives in the now.

We still had 10 seconds left so we had to kick off. Wally dinked the kickoff to my side to confuse Holy Angels. The Holy Angels guy caught the bouncing ball and wanted to lateral back to one of their jet engines but Tim and I tackled him and the game was over.

As we rested before the next game with St. Catherine's, I asked Tony why he threw such a bad pass at me.

He said, "I did that on purpose. Blinkeye or Dana would have caught up to you by the time you got to the 50. Then we couldn't do the fake punt because we would have a first down. When you got a hand on it, if you caught that pass, we lose the game."

When Tony told me that my contribution to winning was that I didn't screw up, I guessed I could leave my superhero costume in the closet.

Our joy over our victory lasted until the kickoff with St. Catherine's for the City title. From the moment they pulled into the parking lot with their new, shiny bus that made St. Thomas' bus look like war surplus, we knew this was trouble. They had the look of a high school team.

As they unloaded, our jaws dropped at the number of extra-large players they had. We saw how they stomped St. Monica's and knew we needed a lot of big plays to stand a chance. St. Catherine's defense did not give up big plays. Their defense manhandled us and we couldn't use our speed due to their superior size. And, furthermore, they were some tough white guys.

On offense, they had a fullback that was a piece of highway construction equipment with a jersey on. His name was Billy Bust and he was almost impossible for one guy to tackle. If you hit him high, you just bounced off. If you tried to tackle him around the knees, most likely you would get run over and hurt. After a few tackles, my arms were numb from getting kicked, cleated, and stepped on. I got a few good kicks to my head and I started to think of the song, "Big Bad John." We started calling Bust, "Big Bad John." Maybe Big Bad John escaped from that coal mine after all and now he's the fullback for St. Catherine's. After one tackle attempt, I had kind of bad vision and looked at the scoreboard and thought their name was St. Coalminers. Wally made a joke that their bus was beating up our bus in the parking lot. I started to laugh, then stopped. I thought it might be true. The rest of the game was a blur. I didn't feel right until we went to Steak 'n Shake and ate after the game.

We got beat by a much better team and everybody was happy to come in second, except Tony and his dad. Tony's dad didn't even want to talk about our season because he thought he failed as a coach because we didn't win City.

The end of the season isn't all bad news. The Knights of Columbus are going to buy new jerseys with numbers on them for next year's team.

So we got to keep our jerseys.

ELEVEN

Secret Agent

Wally asked me to go to Mr. Sauerkraut's house and try to buy the dog that Wally nicknamed "Lookout." The dog was chained to a tree and could barely move because of a short chain. He sat in a box with one side missing just looking out. If somebody approached the house, he barked, growled, and went crazy. Lookout was chained up and lived in the yard all day and night, rain or shine. I didn't know a German Shepherd could be all black.

Wally would go up to $100 but he wanted me to start at $50 and bargain from there. A $100 is a lot of money for a dog, but Wally likes dogs more than most people. Lookout barked at me like a vicious dog when I went up to the door. I decided to tell Mr. Sauerkraut that I needed a dog for protection. (Wally nicknamed the owner Mr. Sauerkraut because he was a German who stunk.)

Mr. Sauerkraut opened the door and I was greeted by his stink.

He was a fat slob in a dirty t-shirt with a glass of wine in one hand.

I offered to buy Lookout for $50 but he said, "Blondie is not for sale."

I went straight to offering him the $100 but he didn't bite. I've seen this slob before but I am not sure where.

I thought I had this guy figured out so I went to the old trick, the "bigot rope-a-dope."

I started, "I wish you could think about selling the dog. It's getting pretty dark in the neighborhood and I need a tough dog in case the 'natives' get restless. You're an adult, you can get another dog easy."

He bit on the bait and swallowed the hook.

He started his rant, "You'll need more than a dog. There will soon be a war where the 'coons,' their 'catlicker' buddies, and all the Jewish swine will be eliminated."

His bigot brain was sparkin'. He got going about Catholic girls being "loose" because they can go to confession. He went off about white people floating and colored sinking and the Jews were out to get Hitler. This was a once in a lifetime creep. I got a little case of goosebumps. I've met a lot of bigots but never somebody like this. I don't want to make eye contact with this creep. He was really happy to share his ignorance with me. He filled a wine glass and kept waving his arms and almost foaming at the mouth.

I saw an "O" tattooed on his arm by his armpit, but decided it was a zero which fit this loser perfectly.

I did a final sales pitch for Blondie.

Mr. Sauerkraut said, "I'll think about it."

Realistically, he should have said, "I'll drink more wine, scratch my ass to kick start my brain, and see how many stupid ideas I can shoehorn into my worm size brain."

I don't think my bigot "buddy" will let the dog go.

So Wally needs a plan B.

I don't have any trouble disliking some adults. Many are worse
than kids and I don't enjoy being around them. We've had many
bad babysitters who sometimes live in my house for weeks. Some
of them are mean women who smell like booze all day. Our worst
babysitter was Griselda. As the day went on she got drunker and
drunker. After dinner she would chase us around with a big leather
belt and try to whip us. She was a slow-moving rhinoceros and
usually us nimble kids could run past her or dodge her. One night
my sister Susan froze and Griselda was able to corner her. Susan got
whipped pretty good for a while until she escaped. We sent letters to
Mom and Dad asking them to come home, but they didn't.

So we were on our own.

46th Street

TWELVE

Zero Plus Zero Is One Big Zero

I was hungry so I decided to get a cheeseburger at the Vu. I was cutting through Butler using the gate by the fieldhouse. From this vista, I saw Chester's Corvette at the Vu. I'm not sure he could recognize me because I had my helmet on when I first met him, but I decided nevertheless to wait until he left. As he pulled away, he went over the bridge toward Wally's paper route. I decided to trail him.

He went straight to Mr. Sauerkraut's house and pulled into the garage behind the house. The dog was chained as always and went crazy barking and snarling when Chester entered the yard. Chester was annoyed that the dog barked at him so he flicked his lit cig and hit the dog with it. The butt bounced off the neck of the dog, causing him to yelp.

Chester shrieked, "Shut up!"

I had a flashback about that time at the Vu when he flicked his cigarette at me. I felt like he really wanted to spit on me but knew that was over the line, even for him. I would never allow anybody of any size to spit on me, but obviously he had his spit on the cigarette so in a way he was attempting to spit on me. Same old big mouth with the same old lit cigarette tricks.

It's funny that Chester and Mr. Sauerkraut have found each other. They are truly "birds of a feather"—two of the biggest idiots in the history of Indianapolis. One has a zero inside his brain and the other has a zero on his arm.

Zero plus zero is one big zero!

I told Meem, my grandmother, about these two losers. When I told her Mr. Chesterfield was a young punk driving around with his Confederate flag license plate, I hit a nerve. Meem told me that back in the 1950s, she was shaken down by some Southern cops who said she was speeding, but Meem wasn't.

Meem said, "I'd rather walk through the slums of Cairo with my purse open than ever go to the South again."

One cop called Meem "Mackerel Mouth" and stole her new tires.

I see white Southerners on TV, spitting on colored kids going to school. These Southerners need to learn some manners. If I was president, I wouldn't let Southerners vote until they stop the spitting crap. Meem says the Southerners enjoy being bigots and admire the Ku Klux Klan goons in their pointy dunce hoods.

Meem also told me, "Never drive in the South, day or night, with a St. Christopher's statue on your dashboard."

We've had a lot of ups and downs at my house, so Meem helps out a lot. When Dad is on the road, and Meem isn't here, I have to solve all the problems that Mom can't. If Meem is with us, I know she will handle whatever comes up. Then I can relax.

One time last year in the middle of the night, Mom woke me up. She said somebody was trying to break into the porch and I needed to do something. I took a second to wake up. At the beginning I was scared because Mom was scared. She left and locked her bedroom door. I had my baseball bat by my bed. I stayed in my room, pumping myself up, until the fear turned into anger. I started going down the back stairs. The house was dark.

I kept telling myself, "Hit him in the head and don't miss."

I kept repeating it in my mind, "Hit him in the head and don't miss."

I stopped at the bottom of the stairs and listened, but didn't hear anything. I entered the kitchen and could see the porch door was still closed. I moved through the house like a shadow and thank God nobody was there. The whole thing was like a dream.

I went upstairs and knocked on Mom's door and said, "It's OK, he's dead; I got him" and went back to sleep.

THIRTEEN

Wrong Woman, Wrong Time

Tony and I were throwing a pee wee football across Illinois Street. On a high arc from yard to yard. We've done it a million times but this time our new police jerk, Officer Tode, drove by and stopped. He got out of his car on my side of the street and told me to stop throwing the football.

I wasn't happy that he was ordering me around so I asked him, "Why."

I knew this would set him off. Tony came over to my side and as he was crossing the street he cut in front of a car that honked at him.

When Tony got near Tode and me he announced, "What's the problem?"

Tode and Tony are about the same size but Tode is much fatter.

Tode seemed to get nervous when Tony came near him and he put his hand on his holstered gun and told Tony and me to get into the back seat of his police car. When we got in, he slammed the door. My first thought was to open up the other door and start running. But

I looked and there weren't handles to open the door.

Tony and I were trapped.

I've had a few run-ins with Tode already. One time he saw me coming out of Hamaker's and he motioned for me to come to his car. When I got there he asked me if "Boney" was one of the seven dwarfs. Then he started laughing and drove off. It took me awhile to figure out that he insulted me. I thought you had to pass some kind of intelligence test to be a cop. Maybe he had somebody else take the test for him.

Tode told us he was going to arrest us, but this time only he will release us to the custody of our parents. He asked Tony his address. We drove there and we pulled up in front of Tony's house. We could see Mrs. Lyons coming out of the house. She rushed past Tode and ran straight to the police cruiser. She opened the back door and let us out.

I was mad and Tony was embarrassed. "We didn't do anything."

Mrs. Lyons turned her attention to Tode.

"Why did you put my son and his friend into the back seat of your police car like they were criminals?"

Mrs Lyons' was angry and talking louder now. Tode made a mistake of telling Mrs. Lyons, "You better lower your voice or you'll end up there too."

"Why did you lock these boys up in the back seat?"

"I caught them recklessly jaywalking."

Mrs Lyons was really mad now.

She told Tode, "Get real, Let me tell you two things. The sun will rise tomorrow morning and if you ever treat any of my children like criminals, you'll have to deal with me."

"Is that a threat?"

"Nope, It's maternal love, honey."

"OK, I've heard enough and you're under arrest. You can hang out with all the other good mothers in jail."

Mrs. Lyons was between Tony and I with her left hand on my head and the right hand on Tony's shoulder. Tode was right in front of us.

That was like dropping a bomb. I saw Tony start to move to his right. Tode went for the handcuffs on his belt. Tony was getting room to throw a punch. I wanted to do something but couldn't think what to do.

Tony was about to explode. There was no way in the world that Tony was going to let Tode handcuff his mother. I started to get ready to fight and thought I would kick Tode in the nuts as hard as I could. I was worried about what was going to happen until I started to feel like my heart was pumping hot blood into my head. My neck was hot.

Somebody yelled, "Hey, what's going on there?"

Thank God it was Fr. Munshower.

"She's under arrest." Tode snorted.

Father Munshower took control. "No, no that can't be right. You just think she is under arrest because you're upset. Are you Officer Tode? I've been hoping to meet you. I heard that you were the first cop on the scene at Rabbi Foxman's accident. Are you free tomorrow for lunch? I'd like to talk to you about it. Can you come by the rectory at noon?"

Tode said, "I can come by but she's still under arrest."

"Great," Fr. Munshower answered and he started to push the three of us back toward the house.

"She not under arrest, I can vouch for her."

We got back into the house and Tode drove off. We filled Fr. Munshower in on what happened. Mrs. Lyons was still hot. Tony was still worked up too. I always hated Tode so I wasn't that different.

Fr. Munshower told Mrs. Lyons, "Let me handle this. I don't think you will look good in stripes."

And that was how we left it that day.

The Canal

FOURTEEN

Bruno And His Rabbi's Death

Bruno was a nice guy who worked at the Shell gas station. He was a little guy, like me, who called me "Master Steichen" with his German accent. Our neighborhood had a lot of Eastern Block refugees, who had been sponsored by churches. They moved here to escape from behind the Iron Curtain. I didn't have a clue about Bruno's life story but it tickled me when he called me "Master Steichen." I felt like royalty, an Indianapolis "Duke of Earl." Jimmy, one of the gas station attendants who used to work at the Phillips 66 station at 49th and Penn, called me "Baby Bruno." He said I look like Bruno. Jimmy was also the guy who thought the funniest thing in the history of the world was: whenever he saw Wally and I together, he always sang, "Pauly, Wally, doodle all the day." I tried not to listen when he was talking.

Wally, Tony, and I went to the Shell station for a candy bar before doing our routes. Bruno was all dressed up. I had never seen him wearing anything but his coveralls. Now, he had on rings, a watch, a nice suit, and shined shoes. He looked smarter and taller.

I went over to him, shook his hand and said, "It's nice to meet Bruno's millionaire twin."

He started to laugh and with a twinkle in his eye said, "I know you know I'm still me, yet."

Bruno liked to joke around and he was funny, but it could be hard to understand his way of talking.

He showed us a story in the paper about a funeral that was today for the rabbi at his church who had been killed by a drunk driver. The driver lost control because of the snow, ran over and killed the rabbi, who was walking his dog behind the Temple. It was a hit and run. There weren't any witnesses but the cops found a full can of beer by the bodies. The cops needed help from the citizens who might have information about what happened or this case might never be solved.

I told Bruno that we were going to investigate the crime scene behind the Temple. He said there was blood all over the snow where they died. Wally heard the "they" part and asked Bruno if the dog got run over, too.

Bruno almost started crying and said, "They are both gone. Everybody always gets killed, even the family dog."

"The rabbi was my cousin. My whole family is gone now. No parents, no sister, no aunts, no uncles, no cousins. It's just me and my wife."

I really didn't understand what he was saying. I think he's upset that none of his relatives are coming to the funeral. I wasn't sure what to say so I just said, "the heck."

Bruno left for the funeral and we went to see the bloody snow later that day.

FIFTEEN
The Hardly Boys

Wally spotted the blood first and stopped his bike a few feet away. It was kind of spooky. Tony made a sign of the cross for protection. None of us had ever been where a person was killed or seen a dead man's blood. There were many footprints in the snow by the blood stains. Must be the cops. You could see the tire tracks in the snow where the car ran off the street for a while, hit the rabbi and his dog, and got back on the street and did the run part of hit and run.

Wally spent time looking at the tire tracks. Tony looked around the blood stains and I went down the hill following the tracks. There was a side street near the bottom of this little hill and the car that ran over Bruno's rabbi turned on this street. There was a bald spot on the side street where a car had been parked during the snowstorm. I went to check it out. I wondered why anyone would park here.

Wally joined me and said, "The car wasn't out of control. He left the road by using a spot where the curb was missing and it looked like the car fishtailed a bit. I think he gassed it and didn't brake."

Tony thought he found the spot where the beer can was. To him it didn't come out of a moving car but was thrown out of a stopped car, and it left a track where it bounced. If he was right, whoever ran over the rabbi came back and threw a full can of beer at him as he died.

We three tried to figure out the area with the missing snow.

Tony offered, "Maybe somebody was necking here like the lover's lane over by Butler pond."

Where the car had sat, there were cigarette butts on both sides. The passenger side had Camel butts and the driver's side had Chesterfields. Some butts were almost buried by snow, while others sat on top of the snow.

"Who would kiss a girl who smokes Camels. Camels are for men," I offered.

Tony guessed somebody sat here in a snowstorm waiting for the rabbi.

Wally looked closely at the tire tread marks in the snow and announced, "The car that sat here made a U-turn, drove up the hill, came up from behind and ran them over on purpose."

We split up and went home for dinner feeling we had done some clever detective work.

Wally went back after dinner with a flashlight and he was going to measure the tire impressions on the side street. As Wally did that, Sammy, his dog, went back to the blood-stained snow. He gave Wally a "come here and check this out" bark. Using his flashlight, Wally could see that someone had put a Suicide skull from the Ron-D-Vu on the rabbi's blood and another one on the dog's blood. The skulls had been painted silver and scared Wally at first.

But then he thought, "Who would do this?" And he knew the answer.

The guy who ran over them was bragging about what he did. Wally got mad and looked around to see if the perpetrator was still around.

Wally felt the skulls were an insult. He found a stick and knocked the skulls off the blood and then kicked them by a bush.

To show how he felt, he peed on the skulls and then told Sammy, "It's your turn."

And so Sammy peed on them too.

When Wally got back to the missing snow spot, he noticed someone had picked up all the cigarette butts. The cops needed to get going on this case.

Hinkle Fieldhouse

SIXTEEN

Life Is One Big Fight

Looks like the world might end soon. My oldest sister, Julia, goes to Marquette and she says the lines going to confession are so long, because people are starting to panic over the Cuba thing. I guess the Russians thought because Kennedy is a Catholic, they could push him around. The paper had a list of the top targets for the Russians, once the missiles start destroying towns. Indianapolis was number eleven on the list. Wally is hoping the Russians will only have ten missiles left, by then.

I've thought about dying and going to heaven when I get old. I never thought of being vaporized as a kid. I'm an altar boy, so I have that in my favor, but I have a hard time following rules that I don't like which will work against me. I think I will go to heaven but not the best part reserved for people with a better record than me. I might be in a mobile home park, down a gravel road on the outskirts of heaven, but I should be there. Most of my friends will be in the same part of heaven as I am.

Meem says worrying doesn't get you anywhere, so I am not worrying on this one. They could miss us and hit Kokomo instead.

Two of the lowlifes in the neighborhood decided to cause me trouble.

I was doing my paper route and they were following behind me, throwing my papers off the porches. I had to go back and put the papers back on the porches where they belonged.

Smeiser was the bigger of the two and I have had many fights with him. His assistant, Rat Face Boy, thinks he is a badass, because he has Smeiser for muscle. Rat Face wouldn't even think about screwing with me if he was alone. Foolishly, I thought at the start the game was them being jerks, but at the last minute I realized the game was them ganging up on me and kicking my ass.

I pretended we were still playing, "hide the newspaper." Rat Face Boy was holding one of my papers behind his back. I pretended I was trying to reach for the paper.

"Come on, give it to me, I'm already late," I begged.

As soon as I got close, I threw a right hook with everything I had. I caught him smack on his temple and knocked him down. He started to sob and whimper. I tried to kick him while he was down, but Smeiser already had gotten behind me and had me in a choke hold. He tightened up his choke hold and I couldn't breathe. Smeiser was bigger than I was, but this worked out for me. I kept squirming and got my feet back on the ground. Then I crouched down a little and judo flipped him. He hit the ground hard. I tried to kick him in the head as hard as I could but I missed and hit his shoulder. I think I heard his collarbone crack. He jumped up like a French acrobat and started running away with his dead arm at his side. Rat Face Boy was still on the ground crying.

I told him, "Get the hell out of here and don't ever come back. If I ever see you or Smeiser, I'm coming after you. You got it, Chief?"

He got up, and for the first time in my life, I kicked somebody's ass.

It felt good, so I kicked his ass twice and told him, "Hear what I say."

Another time, Wally, Tim, and I escaped getting beat up but Pat didn't. I stood on the edge of Buschmann's woods and watched Pat getting punched, kicked, and stomped on. It was hard to watch, but honestly, I was so glad it wasn't me. Better him than me! When I jumped over the hedge as I was escaping, I fell and expected to be pounced on by my pursuers. For some reason, all four of them went after Pat.

Wally ran to the Shell station and yelled to Bruno, "Hide me!"

Bruno threw a greasy, oily tarp over him. Tim hid in the bushes and was scared to death he would be found and beaten.

The four of us were throwing snowballs at cars on Meridian Street from behind Buschmann's bushes. The snow was wet and heavy so the snowballs were wet and heavy. We hit a Corvair that went by with a couple of good shots. As it turned out the Corvair had four Butler guys in it, who took offense at being "balled." They went around the block, and knowing where we were, decided to surprise us by driving to the bushes and hopping out.

Their car was coming down the street toward us when Wally recognized it and shouted, "We already got them."

We all panicked and started running away. The Butler Bruisers jumped out of their car and chased us. I ran like hell and ended up by myself on the other side of the woods.

After some minutes of beating up Pat, the Butler guys stuffed snow into his shirt and pants, kicked him a few more times and left. What great fun for them! For Pat, his nose and mouth were bleeding and his face was swollen and a red color, and it wasn't fun.

When Tony found out what happened, he told us we got out-thought and we should be embarrassed. We had a meeting behind the gas station and made up plans so we'd be prepared next time. We were good at making plans. I pitied the next bunch of Butler boys who tried the same trick on us.

SEVENTEEN

Feygele And Mayzl

I asked my neighbor, Ernie, if he got a big haul of presents for Chanukah. He said although it lasts eight days I get more presents on Christmas than he gets all through Chanukah. I decided to check with Bruno.

When I saw Bruno, I asked him, "Did you get a lot of presents for Chanukah?"

He answered, "I don't remember."

"How could you not remember?" I warned Bruno, "Don't ever let my Dad find out that you can't remember. He won't stop laughing."

I asked Bruno how old he was.

He answered, "I was born in 1933, you do the math."

I did. "So between your childhood and age 29, you lost your memories? What happened?"

Bruno started to tell me a sad story about his family, "I was a twelve-

60

year-old orphan when the war ended. My dad was killed the night we were arrested. My mom, sister, and I got to escape from the concentration camp and hid in France. We were hiding in a hospital run by some French nuns.

"The nuns put a cast over my arm to hide my KZ tattoo. They also put a small cast on my right wrist to confuse the Gestapo. At the beginning of every month, the Gestapo comes through looking for victims. The nuns had a friend who worked as a secretary in the Gestapo office, who secretly told them when the Gestapo planned to come. Before the Nazis arrived, the nuns would put a new cast on me to make it look like I just got there. They also gave me a knockout pill so I wasn't conscious during the Gestapo's tour.

"Everybody says I had a big mouth. One of the nuns was an artist and she painted bruises on my face. This saved my life. My mother and sister pretended to be nuns. The war was almost over and we started to feel good until the last day.

"It was the Gestapo's inspection day and I had already been given my knockout pill. All of a sudden one of the nuns was running down the hallway yelling, 'There's two of them and they have a truck!' I saw my mother and sister in the hallway talking to the Mother Superior. I could hear the Gestapo's noisy boots coming up the stairs. My mother and sister left and I was getting very sleepy. The two Gestapo officers went down the hall in the same direction as my mother and sister.

"The Mother Superior followed the officers and told the Nazis, "Get out of my hospital now. Nobody is going with you. Just leave now." The Nazis laughed and arrested her too. The last memory I have is seeing the Gestapo with their pistols out, taking my mother and sister away.

"As they were hauling them out, I heard the Mother Superior scold the Nazis, "No, no, no, no," and then two shots. Now chaos broke out, screaming and running down the stairs. I never saw what happened that day in the hallway and I never saw my family again. Immediately, two nuns dragged my unconscious body out the back door and gave me to the French Resistance. I think the nuns didn't want me to see my dead mother and sister.

"I tried to find out what happened to them but it's a lost cause. I found a note stuffed inside my cast written by my mother telling me where to meet my family after the war if we got separated, but it doesn't make any sense. The French nun gave my mother the directions in French thinking she spoke it, but she didn't so her translation into German didn't make sense. Mother said it was in code in case the Nazis found it. The note mentioned Indiana. That's why I'm here. I really miss my family. My mother was the sweetest woman that ever lived. She called my sister 'Feygele,' my little bird, and me 'Mayzl,' my little mouse. I got my nickname, Bruno, because I had so many brown sommersprossen. I had so many freckles in the summer, just like your face, that my friends called me Bruno. Bruno means brown skinned in German."

I asked, "Where did your freckles go?"

"I grew over them."

This was the first good news I've heard about getting rid of freckles. After I got over the freckles part of Bruno's story, I realized that what happened to him in World War II is still a torture chamber for him because his voice kept cracking as he told the story.

"Bruno, I know you are Jewish but I'm going to tell you a Catholic secret trick anyway. You need to pray to Saint Jude whose specialty is solving lost causes."

"Isn't Jude a funny name for a Catholic saint?" Bruno asked.

I told him, "I don't know about that, but Saint Jude was a German saint. My grandmother, Meem, told me that Saint Jude never fails. Whatever was lost will be found. Ask Saint Jude to help you find your mom and sister and you will if they are still alive. On Saint Jude's business card it says: Lost causes, no job too big or too small. I'll have Meem pray to Saint Jude for your lost cause, but you need to pray too, for best results."

Bruno didn't know what to say.

"What did your note say?"

It said:

SP
St. Notre Dame Wald Co.
High Land, USA, Indiana

I told Bruno, "Let me think, I know where Highland, Indiana, is. It's near my cousin's house in Munster. Their church is named Our Lady of Something or St. Mary's of Something, and that fits the Notre Dame translation."

Bruno nodded and said, "I know about them but they don't know anything about my mother or sister. Why would the note take me back to this parish?"

I thought I might have solved Bruno's puzzle but it's not that simple. Wald in Germany means woods, but what would Wald Co. mean?

Someday we'll figure this out.

EIGHTEEN

Gutter Ball

Tony spotted the nuns leaving the convent on their way to the church for evening prayers. We were on the DAR roof and hunched down to avoid Sister Mary Jude's gaze. The DAR roof was a great hangout spot. With the exception of an occasional meeting, the building was not used that much. Carter Kane showed me how to climb up the gutters and get on the roof.

The Daughters of the American Revolution (DAR) is a patriotic organization of women. To belong you have to show that your ancestor fought in the American Revolutionary War. My grandmother, Meem, and one of her friends set out to join the DAR years ago. Meem traced back to her great, great, great grandfather who fought in many of the battles during the Revolution, so, she was able to join. Her friend also traced back to an ancestor who fought in the Revolution. Too bad for Meem's friend, her ancestors fought for the British. So she slunk away and never mentioned the DAR again. I don't think there is a DLR (Daughters of the Losing Redcoats).

I really like both of my grandmothers even though they couldn't be more different. Meem has traveled all over the world. She basically knows everything and has done everything. Grandma Steichen was an Irish orphan who is scared of everything. The only time she leaves her house is to go to Mass. She doesn't go to stores, won't ride in a car, didn't go to Mom and Dad's wedding because it was in Dubuque. She is very old. To a lot of kids, grandma is kind of scary and they don't want to touch her. When we go to visit, some of my brothers and sisters won't sleep in the bed that grandpa died in. I don't care. It's just a bed to me.

Some of my sisters think grandma is already dead, but somehow can still move around. She moves so slow that when she leaves the chair by the front window where she sits all day praying the rosary to go eat lunch, by the time she gets to the table it's dinner time.

She still doesn't trust electricity. When there is a storm she unplugs everything in the house, turns off all the electric lights, lights some candles, and sprinkles holy water throughout the house. My uncle says she has an Irish superstition for everything that can happen in life. But I like grandma. Years ago she would wake me up and we would eat breakfast together while everybody else was still sleeping.

My grandfather died early so Meem raised nine children by herself. She was the toughest person I ever met and also the sweetest. In 1956, my family and Meem took a plane flight to California. It was a plane that still had propellers and it seemed like the whole flight was in the middle of a storm. The plane creaked, waving side to side, up and down. People started getting sick. I couldn't sit in my seat any more so I crawled under it. I was bouncing off the floor at times. Some people started to moan and cry when we really got shook good. Most people thought we were going to die. Some prayed out loud and begged God to save us.

Some were yelling, "Jesus, save us!"

I guess they were the Protestants. The Catholics were saying Catholic prayers. I closed my eyes and pretended I was somewhere else. More and more people were throwing up and now the stewardesses were sick, too. So Meem took over. She was going up and down the aisle helping the sick people and calming down the people who were getting overcome with fear. It was dangerous walking down the aisle, and a few times Meem was knocked off her feet when the plane dropped.

One of the stewardesses started to address us on the PA system, but we had a real bad shudder go through the plane and she was too scared to talk. It looked like this would be our last moment on earth and we weren't even on earth. Meem took the microphone from the petrified stewardess.

Meem started, "I have some good news. Now everybody listen. The pilot just told me we are through the rough part of the storm and soon we will be in clean air. There will still be some turbulence, but the rough stuff is behind us. We have a great pilot flying us. Isn't that wonderful?"

Meem just kept on talking, "Wasn't this a crazy flight? They should make a movie about it. If they do, I want to be played by Tallulah Bankhead. Think about who you would have playing you in the movie."

The plane shook as bad as ever but Meem was the guardian angel for the whole plane and she kept talking.

"The pilot told me we might stop in Salt Lake City so we can clean up and change planes. We don't want to arrive in LA smelling and looking like a bunch of wet cats. Everybody can get a hot shower or bath. Wouldn't that feel marvelous? I'm going to have an English lavender bubble bath."

Somehow we got to LA. Meem saved us. She made it up that she had talked to the pilot and we might stop in Salt Lake. Meem limped off the plane but she thought everything was "grand." As we were loading up the cars before leaving the airport, I felt something in my back pants pocket. It was a barf bag that I put there when so many people were throwing up. I thought we might run out of bags so I put one in my pocket in case I got sick. Five of my sisters were in the back two

66

seats of my aunt's station wagon. Before I got in with them, I secretly puffed up the bag to make it look like there was something in the bag.

As I got in I announced, "I brought a souvenir from our flight—a bag of live barf," and I threw it on my sister Mary's lap.

They went bananas and wanted to kill me. This almost made up for the hours of terror we just survived!

Now, let me get back to the nuns walking to pray at the church.

The nuns had made it to the sidewalk as Father Munshower's car was coming down the driveway just ahead. He seemed to pick up some speed coming down the driveway to get ahead of the nuns so he wouldn't have to wait as the procession went by. It's risky business because if he cuts off Sister Mary Jude, he might regret it.

"Thunk!" We heard a loud noise and saw an old car driving on the sidewalk in front of the church. It had one tire on and one tire off the sidewalk and was heading for the nuns. Father Munshower slammed on his brakes when he saw the oncoming car. Father's Dodge Dart stopped when he got to the sidewalk, blocking the nuns. The old car hopped back into the street and gunned its engine.

Father Munshower stepped out of his car and yelled, "Learn to drive, you moron!"

The moron kept on driving and ran the light at 46th Street without slowing at all. I had never seen anything like this guy's wild driving. We started to climb down on the back side of the building when

Wally said, "Quiet!" He was listening for something so we shut up for a second.

"This is hard to believe," Wally announced.

All together we asked, "What is?"

Wally said, "Chester's 'Vette just drove down Capitol Avenue but he wasn't driving it. Somebody who can't drive a high-performance car was driving. They were scared of the power and had a jerky foot on the gas pedal."

I'm sure Wally was right but it was just a noise to me.

By the time we got to the front of the DAR, Father Munshower was driving off and the nuns had turned and started up the church steps.

"Did anybody see the driver?" I asked.

As it turned out, none of us on the roof looked at the driver. I just looked at the nuns. Wally tried to get the license plate number but only could tell it had Illinois plates. Tony wasn't looking, and Tim was surprised and didn't remember much.

We did a pretty poor job of eye witnessing.

Carter Kane had been in front of the DAR so Tony asked him, "Did you see what happened?"

"I saw the part, I saw," Carter answered.

"Did you see the driver?" somebody asked.

"Sure, the guy with the Corvette who lives in Rocky Ripple."

Somebody asked Carter, "How do you know where he lives?"

Carter thought for a bit, then said, "Some things you just know."

We went home wondering what we just saw. Dad was on the road so we got to eat dinner in the sun room and watched TV. I had a turkey TV dinner.

It was fun.

NINETEEN

Surfer Boys

Wally was planning on stealing Mr. Sauerkraut's dog. I told him I would help but the holdup was Wally's mom. She was afraid of big, tough dogs—so Wally needed to make his mother think that a big, black German Shepherd who's been chained to a tree his whole life was not a dangerous dog. "Lookout," as Wally called him, went crazy when anybody came near the house. Sounds vicious to me.

Wally might lose a few fingers over this dog.

Wally sneaked the dog out of the yard while Mr. Sauerkraut and his roommate, Goat Breath, were at work. Wally said Lookout was really smart, but no dog was as smart as Sammy. When Wally was training Lookout, he showed Sammy what to do and then Sammy showed Lookout. The three of them would go over to Butler near the athletic fields to run. The hill that we sled on is there too, so Wally got the idea to teach Lookout how to pull a sled. Then when the snow was really bad, Wally could have Lookout pull him around to deliver his route.

Wally made a harness for Lookout and tied the sled to it with ropes. One day he was at Butler and ran into Coach Bulldog. Coach Bulldog was Butler's basketball coach and this year his team was doing great.

The big star on the team was Jeff Blue. When he was hitting shots, the Butler band would play the song, "Mr. Blue," and the student section would sing along. Wally and I made up a song we called "Mr. Vu," where we sang about "eating French Fries while riding my bike, too—call me Mr. Vu." We practiced at Butler and we all knew Coach Bulldog, who was often around. He was a friendly guy. Coach Bulldog laughed when he saw Wally's setup. Wally told the coach of his plans to become the "Ben-Hur" of paper delivery.

Coach told Wally, "Let me see what you got."

Wally stood on the sled but as soon as Lookout started pulling, he was jerked off. Then he tried to jump onto the moving sled but never got his balance and fell off.

"Are you willing to try something that might help?" Wally nodded.

"Don't think chariot, think surfboard," Coach Bulldog offered.

"What's the Shepherd's name?"

Wally didn't want the coach to find out he had a stolen dog so he clumsily replied, "You mean the dog?"

It was a stupid reply so Coach Tony Bulldog asked, "How many other types of Shepherds do we have here at Butler?"

Wally recovered and answered, "His name is Tony."

Coach Bulldog laughed a bit then told Wally, "Lay on the sled like a surfer on his board waiting for a wave, when Tony gets going at a steady pace, jump up like a surfer and position your feet sideways on the sled and extend your arms for balance. But the key is to bend your knees. Now watch what I do."

The Coach demonstrated and told Wally, "Up—turn—arms—knees—land."

Wally lay on the sled and repeated the instructions. With Coach Bulldog on one side and Sammy on the other, Tony the dog started pulling the sled. The three jogged in tandem and started moving around the running track which was covered with snow. Wally followed the instructions but fell off. He reloaded onto the sled and they tried again. This time Wally got up and was snow surfing. He stayed on until they hit the first turn and he was thrown off.

Coach Bulldog told Wally, "You forgot to lean into the turn. Do you mind if I try?"

The two switched places and Wally got the dogs moving. Tony the dog looked determined and happy. Sammy was barking and Wally was amazed when Coach Bulldog jumped up and started surfing on the sled. He even jumped from side to side like surfers do. He was dancing like Fred Astaire.

Coach Bulldog and Wally took turns riding the wave and in a short time, they were two of the top snow surfers in Indianapolis!

TWENTY

You Think I'm That Stupid?

I served at 7:00 a.m. Mass today with Tony and we talked to Father Munshower about the nuns almost getting run over. He had called the cops to find out if they had found out anything. Patrolman Tode came to the rectory and gave us the story.

He said the cops found the car in the colored part of town. It had been stolen from Tabernacle Presbyterian Church's parking lot two days before the miss and run. The car was left abandoned in front of a fire plug and it had an unopened bottle of Thunderbird wine on the floor mat. When they were towing the car, the cops ran the plates and found out the car was stolen. Since there wasn't a crime committed, the cops were going to close the investigation. Tode said a drunk, colored man stole the car to joy ride. And after losing control in front of the rectory driveway, he got scared and drove back to the colored part of town where he lived.

I had heard enough. "Father, Tode just came up with the most pathetic jive story I ever heard. He is totally wrong. Carter Kane can identify the driver as a white guy from Rocky Ripple. This was a plan that didn't work because you blocked for the nuns."

"Well, you know Carter has a lot of problems," Father Munshower offered.

"Father, Carter's eyes work fine and he knows the truth," I said.

"We don't need a rocket scientist, just an eyewitness."

Carter liked to do things his own way. He had no desire to act like the other boys. We sold concessions at Butler together. Because he is a few years older than I and much bigger, too, Carter got to sell Cokes, a big money maker. I had to sell frosted malts, which was basically ice cream, which didn't sell as well. Selling hot dogs, popcorn, peanuts or cokes were considered a man's job. So I was stuck with frosted malts. We walked up and down the aisles working the crowd. Recently, I was working at CYO Field at an outdoor Cathedral football game and it was 20 degrees outside. On the way there, I envisioned selling coffee, popcorn, or some other big money maker. This was going to be my chance to prove that I can do a man's job. Instead, they had me selling frosted malts, as usual. I wasn't happy but there was nothing I could do.

I went with the laugh option to avoid the cry choice.

After a period of bad sales, where people in the stands were laughing at me, I started announcing, "Red, hot, steamy frosted malts, 32 degrees is a lot warmer than 20."

Then I said, "Frosted malts, guaranteed to warm you up. If you freeze to death eating one of my malts, I'll give you a partial refund."

Slowly, I started to get some sales and had a better night than I expected.

"Carter is not the issue," Tony announced. "The issue is that somebody, not colored, is riding around running over teachers. Remember the rabbi that got run over. Rabbi means teacher, and nuns are teachers. Think about Tode's story. A drunk, colored man leaves a bottle of wine in the car—unlikely."

Tony continued, "And Wally said the car had Illinois plates. I'll bet if that car actually ran over the nuns, it would be long gone. Somebody had a murderous plan on this one."

Father responded, "Let me check it out some more. One of the nuns thought it was on purpose, too."

I responded back, "There is something creepy about Tode. I tried to talk to him about the rabbi that got run over. All he wanted to talk about was throwing me off the DAR roof and handcuffing me. I asked a cop (who had a small vending company that worked with my Dad) about Tode. Dad's cop friend told me Tode's complete name is Frank Lee Tode, and the other cops call him Frank Lee Scarlett or just Scarlett behind his back. His middle name is Lee and he claims he is related to Robert E. Lee. Dad's cop friend said Tode is a snake and he's in the Klan, so stay away."

Then Father changed the topic and told us he had received the football trophy.

"It's nice," he told us.

Tony lamented, "It would have been nicer if it was the championship trophy."

Tony was still stung by our loss.

Father said, "Maybe you guys should have tried the Notre Dame 'Hail Mary' play. It sure worked for them."

Tony asked, "What's that?"

Father proceeded to tell the story. Notre Dame was playing a non-Catholic school from the South way back in the 1920s. The other team was ahead but Notre Dame was about to score. They said a Hail Mary in the huddle before the play and scored. Later in the game, Notre Dame was close to scoring again.

Somebody said, "Let's try the Hail Mary play again."

The team said a Hail Mary and ran the same play and scored again and won the game. The moral is, if you have Our Lady on your side, you won't lose. You can have a Hail Mary pass, a Hail Mary kickoff, or a Hail Mary quarterback sneak. The key is saying a Hail Mary. Ask and ye shall receive.

As we left, Father Munshower promised to get the cops back on the case. Tony told me he wished he had heard of the Hail Mary play before we played St. Catherine's. I hated to burst his bubble but I told him it only works against non-Catholic teams. St. Catherine's could have neutralized our Hail Mary by saying a Hail Mary of their own.

No matter how you sliced it, we weren't meant to be City champs.

TWENTY-ONE

Mr. Lyons Laughing With White Teeth

Tony invited me to dinner at his house. His mom can cook chicken better than Chicken Delight restaurant. Everybody was happy but it seemed Mr. Lyons was thinking of something else. I mentioned that Father Munshower received our runner-up trophy and it looked good. Tony looked at me and shook his head like I said something wrong.

His dad sat straight up in his chair and answered me, "If a second-place trophy looks good, think how great a championship trophy would look."

He wished.

I told Mr. Lyons a championship trophy would look bad to me.

He didn't understand what I was saying and said to me, "How can a championship not be better?"

I told him how I felt, "The only way we could have beaten St. Catherine's is if we had a few better players. Since I'm the worst starter, I could easily be replaced, and instead of playing I'd be standing on

76

the sidelines watching the other guys play. If I didn't play, it wouldn't be my trophy."

Mr. Lyons agreed about being on the sidelines.

He told me, "You deserved your share of the trophy. You played smart and understood your position."

I joked back, "I tried to be the Alfred Einstein of our team."

I think what I just said is the opposite of what Mr. Lyons feels.

To him, the trophy proves we are losers, to me, it proves we are winners. Being a gentleman, Mr. Lyons didn't grill me like Dad would have. Tony's older brother, Mike, thought a change of topic was needed. He brought up that he saw me selling malts at CYO Field the night the Arctic visited Indianapolis. I could tell he was ready to have some fun at my expense, but I was ready for fun, too.

Mike started up on me, "Your frosted malts must have been selling like hot cakes! What flavor icicles were you selling?"

Mike got a few good shots in and provoked chuckling.

I came back on him, "Mike you're good at math. What do you get when you add a 20-degree night, 150 frosted malts, and one top salesman?"

He answered, "Frostbite?"

I answered, "Very clever, I didn't know we had a Jimmy Durante in the house. You know what you get, cold, hard cash."

Mr. Lyons joined in, "Come on, admit that selling frozen malts was pretty ridiculous."

I deadpanned, "What's ridiculous about making money?"

Mr. Lyons said, "You are a true optimist and you just take what life gives you."

I told him, "Mr. Lyons, you're right. I don't expect everything to go right or be perfect. If things work out ninety-five percent of the time, I don't miss the other seven percent when they don't."

I looked around the table but nobody laughed at my joke. I hope they don't think I'm that bad at math.

Then, Mr. Lyons jumped up and had a look in his eye.

He asked me, "If you were a soldier and all you did was drive a truck, wouldn't you think that made you look foolish?"

I answered, "What's foolish about tap dancing on Hitler's head?"

Mr. Lyons remarked. "I don't remember much tap dancing, just truck driving."

I kept the pressure on and told him, "So you ran Hitler over in your big Studebaker truck and then tap danced on his flat head. You won your part of the war just like my Dad won his part."

He said to me, "You're right, you are Alfred Einstein!"

He started to leave the table and Mrs. Lyons asked, "Where are you going?"

Mr. Lyons answered, "I'm looking for my combat tap dancing boots. I'm going to see if I can still fit into my Army uniform."

"Are you crazy?" she asked.

Mr. Lyons had a big laugh and continued laughing out loud, on and off, for the rest of the night. He never came back, and I got an extra piece of chicken. Later, Mrs. Lyons kidded me. She asked if I got

Mr. Lyons excited on purpose to get more chicken. I wished I was so smart to think that far ahead. I told her I wasn't thinking and was really just talking about being on a team and having fun.

TWENTY-TWO

Chester's Snow Cone

With so much good snowball-making snow, the lure of the snowball was overtaking our thoughts. With darkness approaching, we went to the bushes in front of the DAR anxious to start throwing. As we were awaiting our next customer, we saw a Corvette stopped at the light at 46th Street.

I asked Wally, "Is that Chester?"

Wally listened to the sound of his engine and answered, "Yup."

All three of us got loud, good shots on him as he went by.

The 'Vette drove on but Tony said, "He saw us. He's coming back. Let's give him the Butler boy trap."

The key to our plan was to get Chester away from his car so I could deliver a surprise present to him. I hid in the bushes across the driveway from where Tony and Wally were throwing. I was laughing to myself. Chester thinks he is going to kick our ass. I don't think so. Chester drove back from the opposite direction. Tony and Wally started to throw early to let him know we were still there. Looking to chase us, like the Butler Bruisers, he turned into the DAR driveway and pulled up to the bushes. His car skidded to a stop and he jumped out.

Tony stood in the headlights for a second and yelled, "Don't chase me," then ran into the woods with Chester in pursuit.

Wally ran the other way and was long gone.

Quickly, I jumped up and ran to the car with the Kane's snow shovel. I started shoveling street slush from the driveway into his car. I loaded up his dashboard and both seats with dirty snow and slush. Like Popeye, I kept an eye out for Chester's return. I could hear him cussing at Tony from deep in the woods, so I kept shoveling. I turned on his heater full blast and closed the door.

I ran across the street and waited for our "pigeon" to return to his nest. Chester was still cussing and talking about kicking our ass as he walked out of the woods and up to his car.

Mr. Bad Ass is soon going to be Mr. Cold and Wet Ass.

He didn't realize what I had done until he opened his car door. The light came on in the car and he jumped up and howled like a wounded moose. He started to get the snow off the seats with his forearm. Wally hit the side of the 'Vette with a speeding snowball. Tony struck the front window with a loud hit. Chester decided he needed a quick escape.

As he backed up, he yelled at Tony, "You're a dead man!"

Tony yelled back, "Not yet, fool!"

I was still hiding by the church as he drove by. I waved bye-bye. We laughed for a while, then closed our "snowball and snow cone distribution center" and split up.

I saw Bruno and went to talk to him about the family he might not have. I told Meem about Bruno's lost family and she says this will be a tough job for St Jude. Bruno needs to be ready for bad news. Meem asked me if Bruno was married and had kids. I knew he was married but wasn't sure about kids. Meem thinks Bruno needs a family.

I asked him, "Bruno, Do you have any kids?"

"Not quite, yet. My wife goes to a nursing school and wants to concentrate on the school and start a family after she is a graduate."

I felt I needed to explain the facts of life to Bruno.

"Bruno, listen to me .... man to man... Meem says you need a family, now. You need to tell your wife that women can concentrate and be pregnant at the same time. My mom does it all the time. Your wife can do it too. You're lucky that you are Jewish. For a Jewish family you only need two kids. For a Protestant family, you need three or four kids. And for a Catholic family you need seven or eight kids. Tell your wife, 'tonight's the night', and you can have a full size Jewish family in just two years."

Bruno seemed interested and said to me, "I'm not guessing if my wife is adoring your plan but I could be thinking about it."

TWENTY-THREE

O' Christmas Tree

The police cruiser stopped by the woods behind the DAR and sat there in the dark with its lights on. Officer Tode got out with his flashlight and looked at the DAR roof. Then he got back into his car. In the darkness a second car pulled behind the cruiser. It was Mr. Sauerkraut.

Neither of the drivers saw Carter Kane in the tree by the driveway. Carter told me he likes to see how much snow gets on the DAR roof. So he climbed his favorite tree and was up there when the cars arrived. I liked climbing trees, too, but I considered it a summer sport. I mentioned this to Carter, but he pointed out that the view is much nicer without leaves on the trees. I couldn't argue with that.

Carter asked me which I liked better, a winter tree with no leaves or a summer tree with leaves.

I actually thought about it for a second and answered, "Summer trees 'cause they make shade."

He laughed and said, "You're completely wrong. The correct answer is winter trees. Who needs shade in the winter?"

I can't argue with his logic, if logic is what you call it.

The second car's engine and lights were turned off and the driver got into the cruiser with Tode. Carter hid in the tree, motionless. The passenger window cracked open and Carter could now hear the talking in the car.

Tode started yelling at Sauerkraut, "You and Shinola brains' have screwed up everything. He was supposed to stab a nun and he comes back with an ashtray. He's supposed to plant a bomb and he comes back smelling like a skunk peed on his leg. He can't drive. Get rid of him. Let's get the retarded Kane kid. We need to solve this problem with the catlickers."

The police radio now crackled with a call asking Tode for his location.

He answered, "I'm following an intoxicated Negro man who is about ready to mug an elderly white woman on 38th Street. Let me call back in five minutes."

The dispatcher acknowledged with an "over."

The passenger left Tode's cruiser, got into his own car, and drove away. Then Tode drove off. After what Carter heard from his tree perch, he was shaking with fear and his teeth were chattering. Carter had epilepsy and health problems his whole life and knew what feeling bad was like, but this was the worst he ever felt. His body would not follow his brain's instructions. He clung to the tree like a frozen cicada. Finally, his body started to work and he got down to the ground. He sat there to gain strength and stop shaking. Suddenly, he was lit up by lights from a car. He started to panic thinking Tode or the Sauerkraut came back. Thankfully, it was just the sweep of a car's headlights turning into the Shell station.

Once Carter got his legs back, he came over to my house and told me the story. He was jumping out of his skin.

84

"What am I gonna do?"

I told him, "You've heard of having a low profile, but you need to have a 'no' profile and stay out of sight until we get rid of these guys. It's great you heard them because now we know who these losers really are."

Carter was still a worried guy.

I told him, "Chester and Mr. Sauerkraut's days are numbered like an Advent calendar. We are going to kick them out of our neighborhood before Christmas."

I tried to lighten him up with some humor.

" I'm going to order some Christmas trees for us to stick up their asses. What size do you think we need--5 foot--6 foot--7 foot? Do you think the trees would look better if we got flocked trees? You know a flocked tree has that snowy quality I love. If they are out of flocked trees let's get some of the type that rotate and play Christmas songs. That should give them a lot of Christmas spirit."

Finally Carter relaxed and said, "You do that, I'll eat the cookies and milk that they left out for Santa."

"Carter you got the Christmas spirit in a diabolical way. Santa gonna have something special under the tree for you."

I called Tony and told him the news from Carter. I used the same tree up the ass joke but Tony didn't laugh.

He said, "I'll stick these trees up their asses and then pull them out through their mouths."

Tony meant it. It was now time for us to throw the first and last punch. There's nothing we could do about the dirty cop, Tode, but it was time for Chester and Sauerkraut to get theirs.

TWENTY-FOUR

Woody The Snowman

Tonight is high noon.

Tony came up with a plan for Chester and the Sauerkraut. Tony called this one: "The Return to Sender". "These guys came from somewhere, they need to go back there", Tony reasoned. Tony's plan was a variation of the plan we call: "The Sitting Bull." Up until the end, Custer thought he was winning until he was completely not winning and what he thought didn't matter anymore. We'd let our two pigeons think they were calling the shots and we were getting trapped. Then, came the "reversal." We would sucker them to chase us into the woods behind the DAR. And this time not snowballs, but snow rocks. We took golf ball size rocks and packed snow around them to give our snowballs a heart of stone. We prepared almost two hundred snow rocks and hid them under the bushes in the woods.

The property line between the DAR and the woods was marked by a row of 3-foot poles set into the ground and connected by a heavy chain. We used a wrench to loosen the chain and set it on the ground. Our plan was to create a road into the woods that they could use to chase us to get them where we could stone them. Tony wanted to go biblical. Stoning is biblical.

The driveway of the DAR is horseshoe shaped, but we wanted to make it appear like it also went into the woods. We used our bikes to make what looked like tire tracks in the snow going into the woods. The pole that was now in the middle of our road we turned into a snowman we called "Woody." The two poles on the side of our road we painted white to hide them. We took some ashes from the Todd's trash incinerator to highlight the road. Last Halloween, we found a street sign near School #86 that said

"SLOW, CHILDREN PLAYING."

It was stuck to a piece of metal by the side of the road. We were able to get it off the metal with a crescent wrench. We nailed it to a tree by the side of our road. The sign glowed when hit by headlights and really gave our trap a 3D quality. When we were finished, the scene looked like some playful kids had built a big snowman in the middle of the road leading to the woods.

If we can lure these two dinosaurs into our tar pit, tonight will be a good night.

TWENTY-FIVE

Moses Mojo

Tony laid out our final plan.

"We're going to go biblical on them. We'll sucker them into the woods and let them have it. They like to run over people. We'll give them somebody to run over—a Jewish snowman. We'll turn this into a Twilight Zone episode and see if we can shrink their brains."

"My Dad says Mr. Sauerkraut is a Nazi for sure because of his armpit blood-type tattoo. Hitler's dog was named Blondie and, at the end, he poisoned and killed his own dog. The Confederate flag license plate on the front of his car told Chester's story. These guys were two of a kind. They didn't like Catholics, Jews, or colored. Now, we're going to show them what we think of them. It was time for these two to go stink up some other neighborhood."

"We are going to wear some Jewish stars that my dad got in the war."

Tony gave each of us two stars. The stars were new and still had the sales tag on them. Mr. Lyons told Tony he's going to use them in a display with his Purple Heart and other medals. This should fry their little brains. Think of all the power that God gave Moses.

The stars will let Moses know we want him to join our team. There's no Catholic saint quite like Moses. Moses is a Jew, so technically as Catholics we can't pray to Moses for help. With these stars maybe we could get a little Moses mojo going.

When we get them in the woods, or at least behind the DAR, we are going to beat the hell out of them. Our goal was to leave them lying on the ground bleeding like the rabbi and his dog, thinking that they just got hunted down like Eichmann. At this point, we all needed to haul ass.

"That's it. Let's meet after dinner."

Dad wasn't home for dinner, so my night got off to a good start.

Later, we met by Woody. We pinned our stars on both the front and back of us, just like the Nazis made the Jews do, so you could see that they were Jewish, coming and going.

We put a jersey on Woody, using sticks as his arms and he had on his Moses mojo stars. We held hands like a team and said a Hail Mary.

I held Woody's stick hand to include him.

Somebody said, "We better say two, to make sure."

We did and then Tony said, "We have Our Lady to protect us and Moses to help us kick their ass. We can't lose."

We went to our spots, awaiting kickoff.

I had a funny thought.

I thought of a wrestling announcer at a tag team title match introducing the two teams.

Our Lady and Moses taking on Dick the Bruiser and the Crusher.

TWENTY-SIX

Engraved Invitations

The cherry bomb decapitated the mailbox in front of Mr. Sauerkraut's house. This announced the arrival of our invitation. We were now past the point of no return. Guys from our St. Thomas team started the action.

The scarecrow they planted stood there with its sign, "Stay away from St. Thomas, you dirty swine."

I came up with the dirty swine part because I knew it was a German insult. Floyd had planted the scarecrow and threw the lit cherry bomb into the mailbox. Then, he dropped the match onto some hay they had put on the ground around the scarecrow. They had splashed some charcoal lighter fluid on the hay so it took off quick. Nothing quite lights up the midwestern sky like a fiery scarecrow. The scarecrow wasn't on fire, just the hay. Then he ran toward Butler.

Once he got a safe distance away, Floyd started yelling, "Hit the road, Jack—go home—hit the road, Jack."

About this time, Mr. Sauerkraut and the knuckle dragger, Chester, were on the porch and yelled back at Floyd.

Tommy and Richard came from the other direction and pretended they were just rubbernecking. They stood outside and watched as the Sauerkraut read our sign and in a fit of anger kicked over the scarecrow. Mr. Sauerkraut went back into the house and made a phone call as Chester pulled his 'Vette around to the front. The Sauerkraut then charged out of the house with a baseball bat and a billy club. He went around the side yard and came back with his big dog on a chain and the clubs. He put the dog behind the bucket seats and they zoomed off in the snow.

I was waiting in the phone booth. Tommy and Richard ran back to Tommy's house to call me and tell us if Chester and the Sauerkraut were coming.

The phone rang.

Tommy all but yelled, "Here they come, both with a baseball bat and police club."

I answered, "OK, great," to Tommy and he hung up.

I ran to my spot and yelled, "We have liftoff!" to the other guys.

As we awaited our prey, I looked back and saw Bruno answering the phone booth at the Shell station. Normally, Bruno wouldn't answer this. I wondered if it was Tommy again but I couldn't risk going back to see. We had in our plan that if they bring guns or the big dog, it is a no-go and to abandon ship. A lot of the colored guys have bad feelings about German Shepherds because the Southern cops enjoy turning them loose on colored people for no reason, and all of us are scared of a crazy adult with a gun. Tommy didn't mention the dog or the guns but I forgot to ask him to make sure. Maybe our plan is already not working.

We'll know in a minute or two.

TWENTY-SEVEN

The Dummkopf, The Dumb Cop,
And The Dumb Ass Attack

Wally was our bait.

He was easily seen in the bushes in front of the DAR, drawing attention and throwing snowballs. Wally had on his St. Thomas jersey but we didn't put any Moses mojo stars on him. We wanted to save this shock for when the hammer comes down in the woods. He looked like he might have been separated from his herd and was vulnerable now.

Wally planned on looking startled by getting chased and try to escape down the road we made, "The boulevard of broken cars."

We ran some trip wires between certain trees. If the chase went past Woody, Wally would lead them through this minefield at night. Wally and Sammy knew where the wires were. I had snow rocks and some cherry bombs with BBs glued on them. With my sling shot I could shoot them a long way. I also had a military flashlight to use to confuse our guests.

As I waited, I looked at the Jewish star I had on. In the beginning, in the Bible, God was Jewish, and he stayed that way for thousands of years. Then Jesus came along and God became Catholic. Let's hope

God still has good memories of being Jewish and will give us a little Moses mojo. It's smart to borrow Moses from the Jews for this tough job. We've never fought with adult men before.

I couldn't see Wally but all of a sudden, headlights lit up Woody and that part of the woods. Then Wally and Sammy were running into the headlights of the car with the car about a "free throw" behind. They ran past Woody with the car on their asses. The Corvette was sliding on the snow and didn't hit Woody straight on. Still, when the 'Vette hit Woody, the woods shook. Wally kept running into the woods. Our plan worked perfectly until it fell apart.

We were waiting for Chester and Mr. Sauerkraut to get out of the car when I heard Sammy start barking. I looked and saw somebody jump out from behind a tree. Wally was clotheslined as he ran past. I could tell immediately it was the Sauerkraut. He had on his big leather coat and tall boots. Somehow, we let him sneak up on us from behind. Now Wally was on his back on the ground. The Sauerkraut let his dog go so he could strike Wally with the club he had. He cocked his arm back to hit Wally but Sammy bit Sauerkraut hard on the back of the knee above the boot. Sammy was growling and inflicting pain and wouldn't let go of Sauerkraut's knee. Sauerkraut forgot about Wally and looked like he had his club ready to smash Sammy's brains out.

Wally yelled, "Sammy, look out!"

Then Lookout, Sauerkraut's dog, responded by running up to the Sauerkraut and jumping up and clamping his jaws around Sauerkraut's face. They both slid in the snow with Lookout still biting his face and growling. By now, Frankenstein would be embarrassed to have Sauerkraut's so-called face. It looks like Lookout forgot to tell Mr. Sauerkraut that he had switched to Wally's team.

Wally hopped up and started running toward Buschmann's yard.

He yelled, "Sammy! Lookout!"

Both dogs followed Wally into the darkness. Mr. Sauerkraut yelled at them to come back so he could kill them. I used my slingshot and shot a lit cherry bomb which landed close to the Sauerkraut. The force of the blast knocked him down. I stepped out from my bushes and used my flashlight to blind him as he was on the ground.

I yelled at him, "Don't worry about them, worry about me."

Then I turned the flashlight to show off my Jewish star.

"We're here for you, Eichmann. We have a glass box for you in Israel. Master race, my ass. It's time for you to hang. You're going to pay for what you did to the rabbi."

I heard a couple of dog barks and knew Wally was back. And then, sure enough, Wally hit Eichmann with a snow rock that knocked him down as he was trying to get up. Finally, he got up and started walking toward the car lights. He looked like Frankenstein in a foot race to get back to his castle before the townsfolk showed up with torches and pitchforks. He was dragging the leg Sammy bit so well.

By now, Chester had gotten over having his bell rung in his meeting with Woody, and was outside his car mouthing off and swinging his baseball bat.

He warned us, "The first spook that steps on my porch is a dead man."

Maybe his bell is still ringing.

The snow rocks began to arc onto Chester and his car, like arrows at Fort Apache. Thump—thump—thump broken window. Chester just howled like an animal. Somebody got a good shot at him. Eichmann kept slogging toward the car. Although his legs were barely moving, he managed to trip on one of our wires. The Sauerkraut finally made it to just in front of what's left of Woody and I got off a good cherry bomb shot. It exploded just a few feet away. The smoke rose around his body and one of the BBs took out one of the 'Vette's headlights. Both side windows were smashed and the windshield was gone except for some shards in the corners. Chester yelled something at Eichmann and they both got in the car as snow rocks were falling from heaven. Must have felt real good sitting on all that broken glass on the seats.

I taunted them, "Tonight is broken glass night for you. All you can sit on, half price."

They started backing up.

By now we were all out of our hiding places and we were following the 'Vette as it backed up. Wally knocked out the last headlight and we all cheered.

Wally yelled, "Two blind mice, see how they run!"

Sauerkraut, with his so-called face, yelled, "You're all dead! I'll be back with my guns."

They backed onto Illinois Street and almost hit a car that was going by. They started pulling away from us, going faster. But then a fastball snowball came from the bushes by the church and hit Chester smack in the head. Then a rainbow shot that didn't make it to the street. For a second, Chester slumped over the steering wheel, but then he came back to life and they kept moving.

I yelled, "Who's the mackerel mouth now?"

Eichmann was yelling at Chester, "Snell, Snell!"

The engine got louder and the car went faster.

They fled the scene.

We were cheering for ourselves and I headed to see Bruno. Then I heard a frightening crash from down the street. I went to the street and looked toward the noise. I saw a police cruiser stuck in the side of a bus. Mr. And Mrs. Lyons showed up. They were supposed to go to VFW dance and both were dressed for dancing. Mr. Lyons had on his dress army uniform and Mrs. Lyons looked like Jackie Kennedy. Everybody went to see what was going on at the wreck. I might recognize Tode standing by the cruiser.

I still went to see if Bruno would do me a favor.

TWENTY-EIGHT

Turn On Your Lights And The Carhop
Will Come Get Your Tray

The cop, Tode, pulled up to Mr. Sauerkraut's house a few minutes after our cherry bomb took out the mailbox. There were still people standing around by the scarecrow.

Tode looked at the sign on the scarecrow and grunted, "Holy crap."

He threw the scarecrow in the back of his cruiser and started going to St. Thomas. Tommy saw this and ran home to call us.

Tode stopped his car on the way and got a bag out of his trunk. The bag had two small revolvers in it. He stayed on 54th until he turned onto Illinois Street. Now it was a straight shot to St. Thomas. As he was driving, he turned off his headlights so he could sneak up on us. He pulled his .38 out of its holster and checked for bullets as he sped up.

His moment to get us had arrived.

The crooked cop wanted to kill us and plant two little guns on us and say we started the shooting. In his excitement to start shooting, he hurried up and ran the stop sign at 49th. He ran head on into the lightless Corvette that just escaped from us.

The power of the crash sent the Corvette airborne and it landed upside down on the sidewalk. Then the car slid into a fire hydrant and snapped it off. The car ended up on top of the high pressure water gushing out of the broken pipe.

Tode's cruiser careened into the bus. Tode got out of his cruiser and announced, "I had my lights and siren on. It was reckless driving by the Corvette and I'm lucky to be alive. The wreck is all their fault. I had my lights and siren on. We all know that. They're criminals and got what they deserve. We all know that."

When our guys arrived on the scene, Mr Lyons saw the water streaming out of the Corvette.

He instructed our guys, "We need to get the car off that water."

Our guys got on one side and tried to push it off the water. That didn't work.

Tode came over and said, "Get away from that car. They're already dead. It's now a crime scene. They recklessly ran into my car. Don't worry about it. They're goners."

Tony was trying to get a handhold to help flip the car off the water and he yelled at Tode, "You don't know that, shut up and give us a hand."

Tode got mad and reached for his gun. He yelled at Tony. "I'm getting real tired of.."

Mrs. Lyons came up from the side and finished Tode's sentence by adding, "living."

She had Mr. Lyons' .45 pistol and she had it pointed just a few inches from Tode's head.

She warned Tode, "Nobody's going to hurt my Tony, so you need to drop your gun."

It was a stand off.

Tode pointed his gun at Tony and Mrs Lyons' was inches from Tode's head.

"Drop the gun or else," she advised .

He didn't follow her instructions so she said aloud, "Tony, Promise mommy that you will visit her in prison."

That did it.

Tode started shaking and threw his gun on the ground. Mr. Lyons picked up Tode's revolver and tucked it under his belt.

Most of the bus passengers were colored maids going home after working in the richer people's houses.

One of them opened her window and called to Mrs. Lyons, "Girl, I love how that dress looks on you!"

Mrs. Lyons put the .45 into her purse, straightened out her dress and went to talk to her admirer.

Finally, our guys got a grip on the Corvette and flipped it back on to its wheels and away from the arcing water. An ambulance and more and more cop cars showed up.

Fr. Munshower showed up with two detectives from downtown who handcuffed Tode. Tode beat up a burlesque dancer in a motel room. Tode was still mouthing off when he was put in the back of the cop car.

TWENTY-NINE

Alle, Alle, Auch Sind Frei

As I got under the lights of the gas station I noticed that my Jewish star had embroidery on it. I saw the name Jude and knew this was a good sign. Bruno didn't tell me there was a Jewish Saint Jude.

Bruno was closing up the Shell station when I got there. He was standing by the counter that the cash register sat on.

When I came in, he looked at me funny and said, "Your friend rang the phone for such a long time, I answered the phone booth."

Bruno went on, the caller said, "Bad news, a toad is on the road."

I told Bruno, "Bad news for him. I think he just ran into a bus. Bruno, here's the good news - tell your friends at the temple we beat the crap out of the guys who killed the rabbi. It's a Christmas gift from us."

"Bruno, you have to help me. I need an adult to call the convent and get past Sister Mary Jude and get Sister Norbert on the line so I can talk to her. We'll get a cover story for you to use to fool Sister Mary Jude, who always answers the phone. Then when Sister Norbert gets on, pass the phone to me, OK?"

Bruno answered, "You're wishing for my command."

I had to think for a second to come up with a story.

"I got it, you say you have a female cat that's just had kittens and Sister Norbert's cat, Otto, is the father of the litter. You heard that Sister Norbert takes good care of him and you wanted to see if the nuns wanted the pick of the litter."

Bruno didn't think this was a good idea but said, "OK," anyway.

He then told me, "My father's name was Otto."

I told him, "Sister Norbert's father's name was Otto. But don't talk about fathers, just Otto the cat."

He grabbed the phone and I gave him his final instructions.

"Sister Mary Jude is a tough customer. Don't let her crack you, stay with the Otto the cat story till she gives you Sister Norbert."

Bruno seemed up to the challenge and asked for the convent number. I gave him the phone number I had seen on Sister Norbert's arm.

He asked me how I knew that number.

I told him, "Some things you just know."

He told me, "You're the tops. I can only applaud you for your x-ray eyes. Bravo! But you're a little off."

I was confused. He unsnapped the arm of his long-sleeved overalls and slid it up to his elbow. Then he showed me a number on his arm just like Sister Norbert's, same blue color—same poor writing. I grabbed his arm and ran my finger over the number to make sure it wasn't wet. I thought Bruno was pulling a prank on me. Maybe he had been around Jimmy too long. Jimmy was a nice guy but a true dimwit.

I asked Bruno, "Did your Mom write that on you? Mine did on me. What kind of ink did she use? It's not coming off."

Bruno sighed, "That's OK, it's the only thing I have left from when I had a family."

I looked at Bruno's number and asked, "What prefix do the ZZs stand for—Zuider Zee? Zazu?"

Bruno told me, "Those aren't Zs, they are sevens."

I told him, "I know what a seven looks like," and to prove my point I picked up a pen and wrote a seven above each of the Zs on his arm.

He called me, "Mr. Wrong," and took the fountain pen from me and put a line through the two sevens I had written. Now they looked like Zs again, with a tail.

He told me, "Those are German sevens." He then uttered a word like "seven" that begun with a Z.

"So German sevens begin with Z?" I asked.

"Yes, when you see a German seven it begins with Z."

I was tiring of Bruno's runaround. I still had the pen so I crossed out the five at the end of Bruno's number, put a six there, and now his number was just like Sister Norbert's.

"What's this number?" I asked.

"That number belongs to my sister," He answered.

I thought I had him pinned down, so I said, "That's what I'm saying, this is the nun's number, correct?"

He answered, "No."

I then confessed to him, "Bruno, you're confusing me."

He seemed stressed and shot back, "You're confusing yourself, not me."

I still had the pen so I wrote a big letter "C" over the numbers on Bruno's arm and announced, "Like in Tic-Tac-Toe, cat's game, nobody wins!"

"OK, Bruno, I'll give you the number and you dial. The number starts with Z."

Bruno looked like he was going to dial but stopped and said, "I can't find the Z."

I was in a wisenheimer mood so I told Bruno, "Maybe look somewhere near the end of the alphabet."

Bruno repeated, "There's no Z on the dial."

I looked for myself and for some reason the alphabet stopped at Y. I was totally confused, but Bruno looked the convent number up in the phone book. The number didn't have a Z or a 7 in it.

Bruno dialed the number.

I reminded him that he needed to talk to Sister Norbert about Otto the cat. He nodded, "OK."

"Hello, may I talk to Sister Norbert, please?... Yes, this is Bruno from the Shell station. I am calling about Otto, her father."

I waved my arms to get his attention and mouthed the words, "Otto the cat."

Bruno was off the reservation. I should have practiced with him or something. Now he's talking in German. If he was talking to Sister

103

Mary Jude, my future was behind me. I bet that he was blabbing the whole story to her. I just stood there and tried to come up with a plan. I thought this was the last straw for me. Bruno hung up the phone and just sat there.

I asked, 'What happened to Otto the cat?"

Bruno didn't answer. He sat there looking like he saw a ghost. All I could do now was head home and wait for the call kicking me out of St. Thomas.

Out of the corner of my eye, I saw a motion coming up to the glass door. My heart had already sunk, but now it sank to the bottom. It was Sister Mary Jude with her eyes bulging out. She came into the station. She looked at me, then looked at Bruno, then me again. Finally, she chose Bruno, grabbed him and started crying. She was choked up but still was talking in German.

She kept repeating, "My Mayzl."

She took some tears from the side of her nose and tried to clean up the ink on Bruno's arm, but the ink smeared and now you can't see any numbers or letters. Bruno stood stiff, not knowing what to do.

Bruno asked Sister Mary Jude, "Are you a ghost? What does SP mean?"

She answered,

Sisters of Providence
St. Mary of the Woods College
Terre Haute, Indiana, USA

"It means we beat the boots and we're both alive and we're free."

Then she yelled, "Alle, Alle, Auch Sind Frei."

Now, both of them were hugging hard and leaning against the wall, wailing.

Sister Mary Jude told Bruno, "I've a big surprise for you," and they started to leave.

I'm not really sure what I'm seeing. Then, Sister Mary Jude left Bruno. She grabbed me and was hugging and squeezing me. She was crying on my head and saying she was sorry.

She kept repeating, "I'm sorry, I'm sorry."

I wondered, sorry for what? Sorry she didn't have a knife to stab me? Sorry she couldn't have me whipped in front of everyone on the playground? Sorry I was ever born? She cried so many tears on top of my head, once the tears lost their heat, the top of my head got cold.

Finally, she let me go and put the squeeze back on Bruno. They left the station talking in German. Weird! I thought to myself, Bruno never even mentioned Otto the cat.

Outside the convent, I could see a small pack of nuns coming to meet Sister Mary Jude and Bruno on the playground. Bruno didn't know what he was getting into. We will probably find his lifeless body, tied up with rosaries, slapped to death, both ears twisted out of their sockets with his hands pummeled to a bloody pulp with a wooden ruler.

I decided to make my escape before Sister Mary Jude comes back. I did Bruno a favor and turned the lights off and started to walk home.

As I got onto 46th Street, I heard somebody yell, "Paul."

It was Wally and his dogs.

"Have you met my new dog, Snowflake?" Wally asked.

Wally had Snowflake hooked up to the sled.

"I saw you with the Grim Reaper, what did she say?" Wally asked me.

"I think she feels the need to kick me out of St. Thomas but doesn't want me to take it personally. In six months I would be some other school's problem but she can't wait. If it is over, I'm glad it's over. #86 here I come."

Wally announced, "I'll go to School #86, too. We went to #86 for kindergarten and, you know what they say, 'You end up where you start,' plus #86 has a lot of cute girls."

I asked Wally, "I saw that Tode ran into the bus. What else happened?"

Wally was worked up and told me, "Tode ran into Chester's Corvette first and then slid into the bus. The Corvette flipped off the road and landed on top of a fire hydrant. When we got there Mrs. Lyons got upset with Tode and read him the 'riot act'. He got so scared he sprung a leak."

"He peed in his pants?"

"Like a baby." Wally rejoiced.

"That's not all. Fr. Munshower showed up with two cops who arrested Tode.

The cop who handcuffed Tode told the other cop, "Got one that's not toilet trained."

Tode lied and said that he spilled his coffee.

The first cop told the other, "Sounds like he's clumsy, too."

Then he looked at Tode and said, "Nice try, Numb Nuts."

Wally and I laughed so hard the dogs thought we were losing it.

I asked, "What happened to Chester and Mr. Stinkykraut?"

"They drowned."

"What do you mean drowned?"

"I mean too much water and then you die. The high pressure water from the hydrant drowned them"

"Boy, Wally, we thought stoning was biblical justice but Moses went straight to drowning. 49th and Illinois St isn't quite the Red Sea. Maybe Moses brings the Red Sea with him."

As I was digesting what happened, Wally then told me, "Everybody went to Tony's. Let's go and if they have food, stay. Otherwise let's hit the Vu, I'm hungry."

"Slooper Dooper!"

I got the first ride on the sled as we left the woods. The snow was really coming down, now.

We saw Carter back in his tree and he yelled down to us, "Santa wants his cookies and milk!"

I yelled back, "Tell Santa we need to see the presents first before we can talk cookies and milk!"

Every second that went by I seemed to get a little happier. I surfed past the convent with Wally and Sammy jogging beside me. I looked into the convent and saw that Sister Norbert and Sister Mary Jude had their habits off and were talking to Bruno. The three of them had the same red hair and they looked like a family, a mother and her two kids. I guess the "nuns having hair" cat is out of the bag. Sister Damien walked into the room to see what the hubbub was about. She didn't seem to recognize Bruno but his eyes about exploded when he saw her.

He was kissing her hand.

Wally and I could now see into Tony's house through the windows. Mr. Lyons had our trophy in his hands. Then he gave it to Tony, who held it above his head. A handful of Mr. Lyons` Army buddies were there, resigning their war souvenir Nazi flag and laughing about their "moving" experiences in World War II. Mr. Lyons had a friend named Harvey who was a real cut-up. He took the Nazi flag and pretended he was shining his ass with it.

Mr. Lyons joked to Harvey, "I don't think Hitler wants that flag back anymore."

It was a good laugh.

The Thomas Tigers were signing our gift victory football for Earl's mom. It felt like we won City, after all. Mr. Lyons had on his Army uniform and looked like he was ready to march in a veteran's parade. Some of his Army buddies had their uniforms on, too. Mrs. Lyons had on a St. Thomas jersey with pinned-on Jewish stars like the rest of our team. Father Munshower was in there, too. Wally and I left the dogs outside and joined the crowd inside.

I yelled, "Let's all go to the Vu and Father Munshower and Mr. Lyons are treating!"

Everybody laughed but then Father Munshower and Mr. Lyons said, "OK."

Tony led the crowd out of the house and shouted proudly, "St. Thomas, second in the city!"

Father Munshower told us, "We're not going to get a trophy case after all. So, we're going to have a victory parade instead. Let's go!" Somebody changed the "Victory, victory" chant from "Victory, victory is our cry, V-I-C-T O-R-Y," to "Victory, victory we're #2. Not #1, but we're better than you."

Everybody started singing and going crazy. Sister Norbert had her habit hat back on and she opened the window and announced, "No more homework for the rest of the year!"

Bruno looked at me and said, "I am so applauding to you and your teammates. I hope you all live to be 120."

Sister Mary Jude who had on a big smile leaned out the window and announced, "I'm going to be a grandmother!" And then she shrieked for joy.

I looked at Wally and said, "Help me out, Wally, what am I missing?"

Wally guessed back, "Must be some kind of Immaculate Conception."

We both broke out laughing and couldn't stop. I laughed so hard, I couldn't breathe. The nuns were pouring out of the convent, like ants. I looked over and saw Sister Norbert petting Snowflake and Sammy at the same time. Where did her fear of dogs go?

Wally told Sammy, "We're going to the Vu," and Snowflake started pulling the sled.

Ludmila and some other Polish girls from the seventh grade joined us. They started singing a song in Polish. Tony and his mom and dad were jogging together with the trophy. Earl had our victory football and we were throwing it around. His mom is back home and wants us to autograph it for her. The nuns brought up the rear of our surfin' safari and parade.

We chanted, "Victory, victory, we're #2. Not #1, but we're better than you."

When we got to 46th and Capitol, we met Coach Bulldog, who was walking his dog in the snow. He had a real nice looking German Shepherd.

Wally asked him, "What's your Shepherd's name?"

Coach Bulldog, with a sly grin replied, "You mean this dog?"

Wally laughed.

Coach Bulldog continued, "Her name is Natalie. She was born on Christmas last year."

The three dogs were running side by side as if all three were hooked to the sled. Most of the team with our jerseys and Jewish stars moved up behind the sled.

Coach Bulldog asked Wally, "I thought you were from St. Thomas?" as he looked at our Moses mojo stars.

Wally answered, "We are but we needed some Old Testament help for a tough job."

Sister Norbert, Sister Mary Jude, and Bruno had stopped and were back hugging each other in the middle of the street. Bruno really makes friends quick.

I started to howl and say, "Mash good, mash good."

Wally told me, "Calm down, Igor."

I continued, "Mash good." I howled some more.

No matter where I ended up in school, right now, I was happy as you could get. I looked back on the nuns who were bringing up the rear of our parade. In the snow, it looked like we were being chased by penguins.

We chanted, "Victory, victory, we're #2, not #1, but we're better than you."

Sister Damien, the "no, no, no, no" Mother Superior from the French Hospital, heard all the commotion outside and decided to join our victory parade. She hurried up and put on her coat and came outside to join us. By the time she got out, the parade was well down the street.

So she just waved to us and said, "Boy, they're fast."

Back at my house, Dad was asleep on the couch snoring.

Our Christmas tree had a lot of presents under it and Mom and Meem were drinking wine and teaching my sisters how to dance like French girls.

CPSIA information can be obtained
at www.ICGtesting.com
Printed in the USA
BVHW08*0053030718
520656BV00002B/2/P